A Novel

Billie Dureyea Shell

This book is dedicated to:

This Book is dedicated to my nigga
SHAWN FARM nigga I told the next
one would be 2you keep ur head up
nigga we going to get you home........
Just make sure you stop stealing
them car antennas cuz them fingers
was looks bad LMAO Get at me My
Guy..............

Author
Billie Dureyea Shell

Team Shell

ACKNOWLEDGEMENT

This year has really a Mutual Fuckka Co-Vid ain't going nowhere.... But Fucc Co-Vid 19 we ain't going to let it stop NOTHING. So with that let me first and formost give thanks to my heavenly father for making it possible for my family to be okay during this pandemic and for all of us still being here healthy, Lord without you none of this would be possible to my mom I love you with all my heart it's because of you that I'm here and it's because of you that I'll always give 100% , keep my head up and know that I'm the head and not the tail, I love you Momma to my little sister Glenda what's up Blackie I miss you and I love you. To my wife Shatoya thank you for loving me and teaching me how to be more patient I love you with all my heart we got 10 kids you crazy if you think we having another one lol I'm good I got a hold on to the little bit of Sanity I have left smile plus you drive me crazy enough... To All My Children I love you all and know that y'all the reason that I smile to my uncle Woody I miss you and I love you so much thank you for teaching me how to be a man to my brother Lawrence Mc Cloud I love you thanks always having my back to my brother Fred, I told you I was going to do it, to my sister Needra I miss u and love u little sister Bre I always got u...... to my brother and cousin Zane your missed every hour of every second of every day rest in peace we'll be together soon my nigga I got a few more things I got to do down here. To all my readers in the fans I love you all if it wasn't for y'all my dream couldn't have came true thank you for buying my books and reading them thank you all for letting me know how much y'all appreciate my writing skills and what I do its because of y'all that these books can't stay in stores and I'm going to keep on doing this writing shit as long as y'all wanna read it. With that much I'll let u get to this book I hope you all enjoy it let me know what you think I love all y'all

Author

Billie Dureyea Shell

Chapter 1

MAXWELL

When she walked into the room, the smell of her sweet perfume struck me and held me hostage. I watched her move about the penthouse as if they were the only two people here. She wore one of his button-up shirts, a pair of socks, and some boy shorts... nothing I'd allow my lady to wear while walking around in front of my boys. But, my boy Dandridge was different... very confident that his woman was his, and she would never stray. He'd been dating her since our ninth grade year in High School, and I must admit that I'd always been jealous because I'd known and liked her since 2nd grade, but she never noticed me. Even right now, she seemed to be looking straight through me as I sat in their living room, staring at her every move. She sat on his lap and kissed him; I immediately felt myself get angry. "Did you come in here for something?" he asked her, as soon as their kiss had ended. "Just to tell you I love you!" she quipped. "You and Max can finish what you're doing. I'll be in the kitchen making dinner." She was everything. She cooked, she helped their maid keep the house clean, and I'd never heard a negative word come out of her mouth toward him. Dandridge had it made, and he barely acted like he knew it. He played basketball overseas for a team in Spain. He called home quite often to tell me about the women over there, and how his celebrity status always landed him the baddest of them, when he should have been taking the time to notice the bad woman he had at home. Shanice was about 5'6" with a beautiful caramel complexion; her smile was enough to give a man a heart attack on his most confident day. She was shaped like a coke bottle, with curves in all the right places, and her eyes were the prettiest shade of grey I'd ever seen. She had beautiful long curly hair, which I was sure came from her father's side of her family because he was a white man. But no matter where her beauty came from, I was mesmerized every time I saw her. How could a man cheat on a woman as perfect as she was? "So how does it feel to be back, man?" Dan asked, drawing me back from my thoughts. "It's alright... just getting used to being around more often. Looking for a place right now," I answered. "I love moms

...but I'm not big on living with her." My mother loved the fact that I was stationed at Fort Bragg. It was only 30 minutes from her house and whenever I wasn't deployed, she'd allowed me to stay at home, which had saved me a lot of money over the past five years. I was able to pay cash for my ride, a 2014 yellow Camaro, and since I'd gotten back from my second deployment, I was finally looking to buy a house. The only thing I hated was that, while I was advancing in my career and education, I didn't have anyone to share it with. Within the next three months, I'd be pinned Captain, and I'd be finished with my master's program ...and the only woman standing beside me would be my mother. "Finally getting away from mom-dukes! I'm proud of you, becoming a man and shit," he smiled, knowing how I would respond. There was a twinkle in his eye as he flashed me a smile, letting me know he was only teasing. Dandridge had been my best friend so long, he could get away with saying that ...but he also knew when to draw the line. "Watch yourself ...I've been a man. I pay rent there," I corrected him. "I'm not just mooching off of my mom." "I was only joking... chill," he said, looking at me apologetically. Before I could respond, his phone started to vibrate. I glanced over and saw the picture of a beautiful woman displayed on his screen. Underneath the image, I could see the words "The Wife" instead of a name on the caller-id. I had no idea what my boy was getting into, but I knew that, whatever it was, it couldn't be good for Shanice. He excused himself and stepped outside to take the call. "Hey Max, do you want another beer?" Shanice asked, poking her head out of the kitchen, her voice holding me captive for a moment. It was the sweetest voice I'd ever heard, one that I wanted to hear for the rest of my life. There was nothing I didn't love about this woman. "No. I'm okay, Shanice. Thank you," I answered her thoughtfully. "Actually, can you let Dan know I'll get back with him later? I have to run." "Yea, sure," she responded, "I'll tell him. See ya." She patted me on the shoulder, keeping a respectable distance while I secretly enjoyed her fragrance. I couldn't sit there thinking about her being done wrong, and I knew I couldn't have this conversation with him while she was home, so I thought it would be best if I just left, but I would definitely be talking to Dan about the woman whose picture I'd seen on his caller-id. We were boys; we didn't really have many secrets.

Chapter 2

DANDRIDGE

"Look, you know I spend summers at home with my family," I argued with Cecilia. I'd married her two years ago because I enjoyed the thought of having a family stateside as well as having a woman to come home to when I was in Spain. Initially, I'd had no intentions of marrying her ...until I found out she was pregnant with my daughter Danielle. I'd planned on coming home after that season, and coming clean to Shanice about my family, but I could never bring myself to leave her, or tell her something that I knew would kill her inside. She'd been down for me since the ninth grade; no matter what I'd done or what mistakes I made, she never left me. She only loved and encouraged me. "I know, baby," she whined into the phone, "but we miss you ...and I hate going through another pregnancy alone." She dropped a bomb on me! I never wanted kids, never really wanted a wife, and now she was telling me she was pregnant again! "You're pregnant? I thought you'd gotten on birth control! Damnit, Cecilia!" I wanted to curse her out from here to next Sunday, but she was my wife and a woman. My mother raised me to always respect women, especially the one I married. "I thought you'd be happy." She began to cry in an effort to gain my sympathy, but it wasn't working; I needed some time. "Call me tomorrow... I can't talk to you right now." "I love you," she whispered meekly, knowing our conversation would end this way. I forced the words she wanted to hear. "Yeah ...you too," I mumbled as I hung up the phone and tried to regain my composure. How would I explain to Shanice that I would have to go back to Spain early? I loved my time at home with her, and how understanding she was every time I left to go play ball, but I didn't feel like she'd understand an early departure. I put on my best game face as I walked back into the house. I could smell the aroma coming from the kitchen, reminding me of one reason why I loved Shanice so much... the girl could cook her ass off. She'd finished the whole culinary thing, but quit her job as head chef of a very high end restaurant when I told her I wanted to take care of her, and she'd been my stay at home girlfriend ever since. "Umm... sure does smell good in here," I bragged as I grabbed her around the waist from behind, looking over her shoulder into the pot to see what was cooking. "I try," she responded as she turned to kiss me. All I could do in the moment was stare into those beautiful eyes. I had a good woman; I really didn't want to leave early. "What's on your mind?" she questioned, sensing I was troubled. "Nothing... just thinking about how much I love you, and how I want to give you everything you desire and deserve to have," I answered her honestly. "Not everything," she countered. I was not prepared to argue with another woman about the same thing. "Here we go," I sighed, knowing I wasn't in the right mood for this discussion. "Shanice, we've talked about this. I just don't want to be anybody's daddy! I want to know that we can do whatever we want, and not have to worry about a babysitter or kids holding us back. I have explained this a million times." "Yeah, I know," she spoke, the sadness in her voice hurting me to my core. I couldn't continue to lie to her, but I also couldn't lose her by telling the truth.

Chapter 3

MAXWELL

"Hi, I'm Sharon," the realtor said as she smiled broadly, extending a well-manicured hand to greet me. We had spoken numerous times on the telephone but this was our first face to face encounter. "Maxwell," I responded quickly, introducing myself while trying to mask my surprised look. She was sexy as hell and I had feeling that when Dan finally showed up, he'd hit on her, but I could tell that she was already checking me out. I was a far cry from the geeky pecan tan mixed guy no one ever really paid attention to in High School, and truth be told, I could pretty much get any female I wanted. There just weren't any that compared to Shanice. "Do you know how long your friend will be? I have another appointment in a few hours. I don't want to be late," she fretted, glancing around as if she were looking for Dan. "About 10 minutes... he's stuck in traffic on I-40," I informed her, wishing she was a little more relaxed. "Oh okay," she mumbled, but the words didn't match her body language. She was obviously feeling stuck in an awkward position. I'd never been a real big talker, but I figured a little conversation wouldn't hurt to lighten the mood until Dan arrived. I looked at my large feet, and noticed a pebble. Kicking it across the drive, I couldn't help but wonder what made this girl tic. More than just nervous, she lacked the confidence needed in the real estate business. How could a woman so beautiful be insecure? "So, Sharon, are you from here?" I asked, breaking the uncomfortable silence. "North Carolina, yes... but Fayetteville, no. I'm from Greensboro... moved here when I started going to North Carolina Central," she responded quickly, as if relieved that I had asked a question first. She'd given me more information than I'd asked for, though. I never understood why women did that. You ask a simple yes or no question and they give you details on why they said yes or why they said no. I just wanted her to simply answer my question. "Sounds good," I responded. What else could I say? I eyed her for a moment, taking in her 5'4" height, flawless brown skin, beautiful almond shaped eyes, and very pretty smile. She was also dressed to kill, which I find very attractive, so why wasn't I interested in what she had to say? "You seem nervous," I added, deciding to challenge her a little. "Oh no, I'm not nervous," she lied, "just anxious to show the house is all." Looking into her eyes, I knew she was attracted to me because it was very hard for her to act natural. Maybe this girl's not insecure at all... Before I could respond, the moment disappeared with the arrival of Dan's white on white 2013 Yukon Denali. His music was loud as always, blaring Jay-Z's Run This Town ft. Rihanna. Dan seemed go for the 'I need attention' effect in everything he did. "Hey! Sorry I'm late," he said, stepping out of the car to extend his hand to Sharon. "I'm Dan." I'd seen that smile enough times to know that he'd be laying on the charm for this girl. Resisting the urge to shake my head in disapproval, I responded before Sharon had the opportunity. "It's cool Bruh, come on. Let's look at this house." Sharon led us into the beautiful four bedroom, three and a half bath, plantation style home, it's modern touches included hardwood floors, black granite counter tops, a range stove, and luxury his and hers shower heads in the master bath. It was a home fit for the family I planned to have one day. "Why would you buy a house this big, man?" Dan asked, looking at me as if my viewing this home was one of the craziest things he'd ever heard, "it's just you..." "I do plan to have a wife and kids one day," I explained, looking at Dan as if he were crazy. Was he serious …or just trying to be smooth in front of this girl? I wanted to say something else to defend myself but he continued. "You don't think you should wait till that happens so your wife can pick out your family home with you?" His question made sense, I guess, but since when did Dan start thinking of what his wife would want, anyway? "Sharon, what do you think? Do you think I should go smaller and then upgrade when I find a wife?" I could tell I'd caught her off guard, including her in our conversation but I wanted insight from a female perspective. "I personally wouldn't mind moving into a home my man already purchased, especially if it was a home as nice as this. That's one less thing we'd have to worry about financially." She smiled and I almost melted. "Whatever, man! You think you want a wife and kids one day, but it's not all it cracked up to be. Buy your invisible family this house if you want to," Dan sounded like a bitter, jaded old man. He threw his hands up and walked swiftly into the other room. Something was obviously bothering him. I asked Sharon to give me a minute to look through the house again, although I'd already made up my mind. I just needed time to speak to my boy. He'd been easy to find, standing on the veranda with one hand on his hip and the other leaned against the pillar. "What's up, man? What do you know about having a family?" I asked. "Sure, you've got Shanice, but that's hardly the same as a wife and kids." "I messed up, bruh! I messed up bad… and the situation is getting harder and harder to keep under control." He put his hand to his forehead to think, but then brought it down again as if trying to regain his composure. "What situation?" I could tell by his nervousness and body language that whatever he had gotten himself into wasn't good, but I wasn't prepared for his response. "I married a girl in Spain," he confessed. "We have a two year daughter and now, there's a baby on the way." "You're joking!" I responded, laughing because I honestly thought he was joking until I saw the look in his eyes. "I wouldn't play about nothing like this, man," he hissed quietly, looking behind me to make sure no one could hear, "but the problem is, my family has never really approved of Shanice. They love Cecilia and our daughter… but I love Shanice more than life, bro." His eyes looked watery, as if he were on the verge of tears. "If you loved her, you wouldn't be in this predicament, man," I replied, knowing my words would fall on deaf ears. He was obviously distraught but there was no real remorse in his voice. I honestly wanted to beat him to a bloody pulp but controlled the anger I felt. "You need to tell her the truth." "I can't do that… I can't hurt her like that," he whined, sounding more and more selfish with each word he spoke. He'd rather live a double life than allow Shanice to have the love and happiness she deserved. "I just have to figure out how to tell her I'm leaving for Spain in three weeks because I can't let my wife go through this pregnancy without me!" Before I could say anything, Sharon stepped onto the veranda. "So, have you decided yet?" she asked politely. Dan looked away, smoothing his collar and trying to compose his thoughts. "Yes, I'm going to put in an offer," I announced. It seemed as if my invisible family might materialize sooner than I had originally expected.

Chapter 4

DANDRIDGE

I looked up at the ceiling while Shanice slept peacefully on my chest. I didn't know how I had allowed myself to get into this situation. Caught between two women I cared deeply for, and destined to hurt the one I loved most. Shanice was an amazing woman and she deserved the world, but I knew I'd never be able to give her all that she wanted ...because I'd mistakenly given it to another woman. My relationship with Cecilia started out as a 'friends with benefits' situation. I'd come back to my hotel room one night and she had been a gift from the boys, but there was something different about her. She was beautiful and actually very smart. The first night we spent together, we stayed up late, talking until we fell asleep, and made love in the morning. Cecilia had done some things to me that I only dreamed Shanice would do, but because I was the only man Shanice had been with, she was still rather conservative, which was the only reason I'd sleep with other women. I started inviting Cecilia to home games and bringing her along for the away games. We connected in an indescribable way. I had never considered her my girlfriend but when she popped up pregnant, my mother told me that I needed to leave Shanice alone, and make an honest woman out of the Cecilia, the woman having my child. So, I proposed and two months before she'd given birth to Danielle, we had a small wedding with only our closet family members... none of our friends had been invited. I was still shocked to this day that no one in my family had taken it upon themselves to tell Shanice, but my sister has always said it was my place to be honest with her ...not anyone else's, even though my mom seemed anxious to tell her. I looked down at Shanice. She was so beautiful, sleeping like there was no place she'd rather be. I knew this wasn't the time, but I had to wake her and tell her the truth ...before I lost my nerve. "Yes?" she said without opening her eyes when I shook her awake. I would have found that comical if the situation were different. She's always been bad about answering when she's still sound asleep. "Wake up, babe," I said kindly, urging her to open her eyes, "I need to talk to you." "Now?" she asked quietly. I could tell by her voice that she was bothered that I'd chosen to wake her. "Yes, it's important." She lifted up off of me and propped herself on one elbow so she could face me as I spoke. The moonlight shone through the window, adding the perfect reflection of light. Now that I was able to see those beautiful grey eyes of hers, I lost my nerve. "Okay babe, you have my attention," she said, realizing that I hadn't said anything yet. My thoughts stumbled, looking for the words that would send her back into a peaceful sleep. "I just wanted to say I love you more than life itself, and no matter what, I never want to lose what we have. I never want to lose you." "And you never will," she answered sweetly, "as long as you're always honest with me and faithful to me." She looked at me as if searching for clues of deceit and betrayal. "I would never lie or cheat," I lied. Trying to lighten the mood, I added with a grin, "you've been down for a nigga for too long." "You better not," she said in her most menacing tone as she leaned in and gave me the sweetest kiss. I loved this woman... she was every man's dream.

Chapter 5

MAXWELL

I sat down for Sunday dinner with my mom. It was always just the two of us since before I could remember. My dad had run off with some white woman and had five other kids that he raised, all the while acting like I never existed. But it was okay, I didn't need him. I'd always had my mother to teach me how to be a successful person, a man she could be proud of. «So, when am I going to meet this girl you went out with?" she immediately asked the moment I'd sat down. "You're not," I smiled, taking a big bite to pause our conversation. I knew my mother hated that she'd never met one female I was involved with, but it was for a damn good reason. There was no use in introducing my mother to someone who wasn't Shanice. Most people thought that, because I was a sexy and successful black man that I was probably going out, and having sex with any woman who was willing. In reality, I was 25 years old and had only had sex with one woman. After a failed relationship during my first deployment, I made a vow to myself and to God that I would no longer share myself with meaningless women. I would wait on my wife, and I prayed that the wait would bring me the woman I'd always hoped for, beautiful inside and out. "Well, can you at least tell me about her? You never tell me anything about your dating life, Max." My mom sounded hurt that I'd excluded her from that aspect of my life. "Her name is Sharon, mom. She's beautiful, successful, and very sweet, but I can only see friendship coming from us hanging out." I spoke honestly. I'd asked Sharon out after I closed on the house, which I still hadn't mentioned to my mom. She was used to having me around and now her baby boy was leaving. I honestly hoped my moving out would open the door for her to date again. She deserved a good guy. "What's wrong with her? You just described a good woman," she asked, looking at me with a confused and suspicious look, "so, what are you not telling me?" "She's just a little too timid for my taste," I lied. The only thing standing in the way of me seriously giving Sharon a chance was my love for Shanice, but my mother didn't need to know that. "She's your best friend's girlfriend." My mother caught me completely off guard, making my heart skip a beat.

How had she known? All I could do was pretend not to know what she was talking about. "What? Who are you talking about?" I asked, unconvincingly. "I found a picture in your room the other day. It's a picture of you, Dan, and Shanice. The way you're looking at her in this picture, there is nothing but love in your eyes. But be careful son, the love of that woman comes at the price of a friendship. You sure that's a price you're willing to pay?" she said, looking at me with all seriousness. "I'd pay any price to be the man she needs," I answered, letting her know how deeply I felt for the girl. "Alright, but don't say I didn't warn you! Betrayal is something you can't come back from, son." And with that we ate silently. All I could do was think about my mother's warning, but Dandridge had already demonstrated the ultimate betrayal to Shanice when he married another woman behind her back. He deserved his fate, whatever it held, and I couldn't help but hope for my own happiness now.

Chapter 6

DANDRIDGE.

"I>m not okay with this,» Shanice said sternly, as we stood in my mother's living room. I>d told her that the coach wanted to do more extensive training and I>d have to go back sooner than we>d expected. "I don>t have a choice. You think I>d just choose to go back? This is our only source of income so unless you want to give up those designer clothes, shoes, and purses, I suggest you jump on board and support me.» I knew I was wrong for trying to make her feel bad for wanting me to stay, but I didn>t know what other route to take. "You know I don't care about that shit, Dandridge! All I want is the time I was supposed to have with you," she pouted. "You'd care if your ass was living on the streets somewhere," my mother barked, interrupting the argument we were having.

"Mom, please..." "Don't you mom please me! This girl has been riding your coat tail since high school and you're just too foolish to see it, but I know a gold digging hoochie when I see one." My mother's words were always like daggers when it came to Shanice. "Well, it takes one to know one!" Shanice spit venom right back at her! "Wait a minute, Shanice. You will not speak to my mother that way!" I saw this situation getting real ugly, real fast, and I knew I had to stop it. "Don't speak to your mother that way? Really Dan? This woman has been disrespecting me since high school, and for what? Because my family doesn't have as much money as your father has? This bitch hasn't worked a day in her life," she retaliated. Shanice had stepped so far out of character that even I didn't know what to say, but my mother was on it without missing a beat. "Listen little girl, you might think that because you're grown now that you can disrespect me in my house, but you better watch it before somebody gets hurt. You think basketball is the only thing waiting for my son in Spain?" "Mom!" I said, raising my voice to cut her off before she could say anything more. "That's enough!" I turned to Shanice, who was now staring a hole through me, her beautiful gray eyes fierce with rage. "Is there another woman?" she demanded. As the question left her lips, I was relieved to see my boy Maxwell walk in, just in time to save me. "Hey everybody, I brought a bottle of…" His words trailed off when he felt the tension in the room and noticed the expression on Shanice's face. Max froze, holding the bottle of wine. "Is… there… another woman?" Shanice demanded again, her eyes now filled with tears. There was no way I could embarrass her in front of everyone. "No, baby… there is no one else," I lied, looking directly into her eyes in an effort to relieve her worries and fears about my fidelity. "My mom just wanted to get a rise out of you. I told you, babe. I'd never lie to you or cheat on you." I pulled her into my arms to offer her reassurance, and for the first time, I'd noticed a look in Max's eyes that I hadn't seen before. It was a look of fury, but I had no idea why he'd be so angry. "Humph!" I heard my mom say, as she walked through the doors to enter the kitchen. Everyone knew the truth except Shanice, and I intended to keep it that way.

Chapter 7

MAXWELL

I wanted to punch Dan in his throat for lying to Shanice when he had been given the perfect opportunity to tell her that, not only was there another woman, but that this woman was his wife. I sat on the couch silently, listening to him as he consoled her... telling her how much he loved her and how sorry he was for allowing Mrs. Harris to disrespect her. I couldn't believe Mrs. Harris had the nerve to continue to treat Shanice the way she did, especially after the way her son had deceived this girl. They'd come from the same projects and both just so happened to be the apple of a Harris man's eye. Mrs. Harris, whose real name was La'Draysha Barnes, met Dandridge Harris Sr. at a local club when they were in college. She latched onto him because his family owned one of the top legal firms in North

Carolina dealing in family law, and she knew he was next in line to take over. His mother never really approved of her because she'd only taken to him because of their wealth, and it was often said around town till this day that Dan might not be his biological son. And yet, Mrs. Harris has the nerve to treat Shanice like she's unworthy. I loved her, but she was dead wrong... just like Dan was dead wrong. "Hey man, I think we're going to cut this bon voyage party short. Want to head over to the bowling alley with us?" Dan asked, taking me away from my thoughts. "Sure man, let's go," I responded, shamelessly wanting more time with Shanice, even if it meant spending time with Dan too. "Aight... let me tell moms and my sisters goodbye." Dan left me standing in the living room with Shanice, who looked like a lost puppy. I silently wished I could hold her and make her feel alright. It bothered me to see her so sad. "Crazy night," I said softly to her, trying to break the silence between us. I wanted to put my arms around her so she didn't feel so alone, but I knew that would be crossing the line. "Yeah, it's always a crazy night when I'm around Mrs. Harris. I just came to support Dan but I guess it didn't turn out so well," she mumbled, shrugging her shoulders. "And she's never going to like me, no matter how much I try...." I laughed an uncomfortable, awkward laugh before leaning slightly toward her, whispering my response so no one would overhear. "No, I guess it didn't, but one of these days, she will regret treating you this way." She looked up, her eyes silently thanking me for the support and kind words, and I enjoyed talking to her alone, while her defenses were down. I couldn't really explain why. "So, what are you going to do when he goes back to Spain?" My curiosity had gotten the best of me. If I couldn't be with her, I needed to know how she spent her time. "Same as always... read as many romance novels as I can get my hands on, and try new recipes. You know, perfect my craft," she answered me, smiling through the pain. "Sounds okay to me," I mused. "Who do you read?" Looking into her eyes was extremely difficult, knowing I couldn't hold or touch her, but I found myself surprisingly interested in everything she had to say. "Some of everybody, really... I love Zane, but I'm also getting into this new author, Christie Anthony. Her books are very good as well!" I watched as she went from sad to excited when I asked about her books, and I was happy that I'd taken her mind away from Dan's foolishness. "Moms didn't want to let me go," Dan announced as he came back into the room smiling, until he noticed that Shanice no longer looked sad. "What's going on in here? What did I miss that has everyone so happy?" he accused, sounding more than a little jealous. "Nothing, man... let's go." I headed toward the door with a satisfied grin on my face. For the first time, I actually felt like she'd noticed me. I wasn't Dan's friend... I was Max. I felt like I had a fighting chance.

Chapter 8

DANDRIDGE

I sat in the airport thinking about how much chaos I'd caused in my own life, and how, for two years now, I'd led Shanice to believe that we had something we really didn't. I'd turned the woman who loved, supported, and encouraged me into my place holding mistress, and she was absolutely clueless. Cecilia was far from being a bad wife but she wasn't Shanice either. Shanice didn't deserve what I'd done to her and that was a fact. I also couldn't shake the feeling I'd had around Max the night prior. He was being extra friendly with Shanice, and acting more like her protector than my best friend. If I didn't know any better, I would have sworn he was flirting with my woman, right in front of my face, but I knew Max wouldn't do that to me, no matter how bad I'd messed up. My FaceTime application started ringing and I already knew it was Shanice. This was something we did every time I traveled. "Miss me already?" I asked as soon as the call connected. "You know it," she quipped, while smiling her flawlessly beautiful smile. "I miss you too baby," I responded, happy to hear from her. I'd been nervous to leave her after the scene at my moms. "I'll be back before you know it." "Maybe before you know it but I'll be counting the days," she told me. There were so many things I'd done wrong, and sitting here now, I realized there was no way to take it all back. All I could do was pray that, when she found out the truth, she loved me enough to forgive my faults. "I think you and my mom should try to make amends while I'm gone, bae. I know it's a lot to ask but I want you in my life forever, so it would mean everything to me for the two of you to finally form a bond. Don't stay away from them like you usually do." "Why mess up a good conversation, Dan?" Shanice scowled, which only made her look even more adorable. "Your mother is never going to approve of me so let's not pretend like forging a bond is so easy to do." "Well, let's make a deal. If the two of you can learn how to get along before I get back, you and I can start planning our future," I lied, instantly regretting my words. Why had I said that? I was making things worse with every minute that passed. "Our future?" she asked, lifting a brow. "This is coming from Mr. I don't ever want to be a husband or a father?" She laughed. "Yeah, right! Baby, board your plane and make sure you call me when you get there. I love you." She had immediately dismissed what I'd said and rightfully so. I was glad that I'd expressed my hate for marriage and kids to the point where, even when I mentioned it, she considered it a joke. I just prayed that nobody would tell her about Cecilia and Danielle before I had the chance, considering how heated things were becoming between her and my mother.

Chapter 9

MAXWELL

I sat at my desk, staring at no particular thing. My mind was so lost in all of the things that were going on with Dan and Shanice that I could barely focus on my own life. The night we went bowling, I'd probably overdone it with how friendly I was being toward Shanice. I wanted her to feel comfortable laughing and talking with me because, when everything did finally blow up in Dan's face, I wanted to be the one she ran to. My phone started ringing, taking me from my thoughts. "Lieutenant Taylor," I answered. "Hey LT, this is SPC Downs. I was just wondering if you'd signed those exception reports for the commander yet?" I heard a soldier on the other end and remembered why I'd been at my desk instead of at the motor maintenance formation in the first place. "I'll be down with them shortly," I told him, so he wouldn't think he needed to come in my office to pick them up. That was pretty much the bulk of my job. I looked over and signed paperwork all day and if something needed fixing, I delegated that task down to the non-commissioned officers and their soldiers. I picked up the phone to see if Sharon was free for lunch. I was waiting on Shanice to fall madly in love with me but there was no use in waiting alone. Plus, Sharon was really good company. "I thought you'd forgotten about me," she answered in a teasing tone. "Oh no, I've just been busy reintegrating back into my unit and getting things done for reset." I spoke to her like she was a soldier and I could tell the reset part went over her head. "I guess," she said softly and I laughed. "I'm sorry," I began. "I'm speaking to you like a soldier but that's not what I was calling for. Wanted to know if you are free for lunch at around 11:30ish?" She hesitated for a moment before she answered. "Max, you're a nice guy and all, but I don't really want to be involved with someone who calls me when he feels like it, and ignores me the rest of the time. I don't really think you and I are looking for the same things." Did she not hear me say I'd been busy? "I'm not trying to lead you on or play games. I also don't know what could happen between us, but if you want to shut it down because I have a demanding job, you're right. We aren't looking for the same things." I was a nice and respectful guy but I wasn't timid, nor was I a pushover and I didn't like her approach. If she wanted to say no, that's all she had to say. I heard silence on her end and decided to look at my phone to make sure we hadn't been disconnected, we hadn't. "Hello?" "Yes, I'll go to lunch with you," I finally heard her say. Women were so difficult; it was ridiculous. I called to ask a simple question and ended up having an entire discussion. They needed to learn that simple answers went a long way.

Chapter 10

SHANICE

walked into the condo I sometimes shared with Dandridge feeling a bit uneasy. After everything that had occurred at his moms place, I really did wonder if Dan was cheating on me again. We'd been together since ninth grade and, over the past eleven years, he'd been caught cheating on more than one occasion but we'd gotten through it. In the last six years, Dan had given me no reason to believe he was back to his old tricks and foolery. I wasn't naïve or stupid... I loved him and was willing to go through the fire with him, but something just wasn't right. I decided to give Dan's mother a call. I knew it was a long shot but if he indeed wanted us to make amends, I was willing to try yet again, but if this lady disrespected me one more time, she might find herself needing a hospital bed. I'd never disrespected his mother until the other night, and only because I'd had enough of being called a gold-diggin' hoochie among all the other names she'd called me over the years. Unlike her, Dan's money had nothing to do with why I loved him. I didn't even know his family had money when we first got together. His mother was upset that, during our senior year in High School, Mr. Harris left her. He told her he couldn't live the lie he'd been living for so long, and since Dan was about to graduate, he could finally enjoy his life with his partner and stop pretending to love her. Dan and his two sisters never judged their father. Even though they were hurt when he left, they just continued to love him and that burned Mrs. Harris up even more. After graduation, Dan attended North Carolina State University on a basketball scholarship, and talked his father into paying my way through Raleigh's Art Institute because my family couldn't afford it. It had caused me a lot of grief with Dan's mom but the degree was worth it. With my scholarship and few grants, I only would have gotten through to my sophomore year. She swore that Mr. Harris' generosity was the only reason I was with her son, and because Dan could give me everything I didn't want to work for. I hated that bitter old woman. And I hated the fact that she was making me bitter too. "Why are you calling me," she answered coldly into the phone. Taking a deep breath, I responded as if she'd greeted my call with a chipper hello. "Well, hello to you too, Mrs. Harris," I chimed in my friendliest voice. I still wondered why her and Dan's father had never actually divorced, just lived separate lives... but that wasn't my business. "Look child, I'm busy so what do you want?" She continued to be rude but I wasn't going to let her get to me this time. "I'm cooking dinner tomorrow night, and wanted to know if you'd come over and eat with me?" I tried to sound unfazed by her attitude. Maybe I was secretly hoping she'd say no and hang up on me, but instead, she hit me with another insult. "Girl, we ain't friends! Don't you have some friends your age... some men you can call?" she quizzed me in an accusing tone. Mrs. Harris was about to cross the line but I decided to try inviting her one more time before throwing the phone. "Yes ma'am. I have female friends." I put extra emphasis on female. "But, I'd like to have dinner with you. Can we put our differences aside for one night?" There was silence on the other end for a moment, causing me to look at the phone to see if we were still connected. The clock was still counting, so I knew she was listening. "Even if you still hate me, I promise you'll love the food," I added. "Ok, what time?" she sighed, obviously put out by my self-control. I was determined that she wouldn't rattle me again, not like she had on Dan's last night home. "How about 8:00?" I asked.

"8:00? Girl, who eats dinner that late? I will be there at five sharp. It's not like you're doing anything anyway, except waiting on the next check to arrive from my son." She hung up the phone before I could agree to the time she'd set. "This woman is going to be the death of me," I said out loud to no one in particular, but the look on our maid Angel's face said she totally agreed.

Chapter 11

MAXWELL

I sat in subway for almost 30 minutes alone, waiting on Sharon to arrive. I was beginning to think she'd stood me up until I saw her speed walking over to my table with her food in hand. I hadn't even noticed her standing the line, maybe because my eyes were glued to my kindle reader as I read Chasing Disaster, that Christie Anthony book. I was going to pull out all the stops when it came to Shanice, and reading the same books as her would be a great start. "You haven't ordered yet?" Sharon asked, feeling a little inconspicuous with her food already in hand. "Oh nah, I was waiting on you. I would have paid for that," I stated, trying not to appear annoyed. "I'm sorry," she began. "I ordered because I thought you'd probably be halfway finished with your meal, considering my tardiness." I gave her a look and, without saying a word, went to order my food. For some reason, Sharon was really getting on my nerves today. I've always gone out of my way to be a complete gentleman. Why would I begin eating before she arrived? That's rude. But I guess it makes sense, since she didn't even have the decency to call and let me know she was running late. After getting over the fact that Sharon was late and had paid for her own meal, we actually had a great lunch. She asked me to explain the reset process to her, and she talked about the house she'd just sold, which was why she was late. I still hadn't started moving my things into the new house because I hadn't figured out how to break the news to my mom. I was sure she'd be alright, but I hated to just up and leave her, knowing she'd be struggling with the bills once I was gone for good. "So, do you know any good interior designers?" I really didn't want to start decorating, and turn my new home into something that looked like a bachelor pad. I wanted my home to have color and character, cheerful and comfortable surroundings for a family. "Actually, my best friend Sue has her own interior design company. Let me see if I have her card on me," she said before turning her attention the the huge duffle-sized Coach purse. I felt like it was going to take her forever and a day to unpack her luggage and find that card. Sharon was extra; who needed a purse that big? Where was she going when she left here ...to the airport? Several minutes had passed before she finally retrieved the card and handed it to me. "Thanks," I said, taking the card from her manicured hand. "I'll be sure to give her a call. I have to get back to work though." "Ok, will I see you later?" she asked, smiling broadly as she stood. As she gathered her belongings, I wondered if others noticed how awkward she looked, carrying that huge bag when she was so petite. "Yeah, I'll give you a call," I promised, hugging her before I disappeared into the street. I honestly had no idea why I was giving Sharon such a hard time. I didn't want her to get too close to me or become too attached. Maybe next time I'd make it clear that I was only trying to build a friendship. If I did that, perhaps I could actually spend time with her without trying to find flaws in everything she said and did.

Chapter 12

DANDRIDGE

"I love you too," I said, hanging up the phone with Shanice, who was nervous about her dinner date with my mom. I'd snuck off into the bathroom just to call her because Cecelia didn't want to give me room to breathe since I'd walked in the house. We owned a four bedroom, three bathroom old style Spanish home. It was beautiful on the inside but from the outside, you'd think someone should tear it down. I told Cecelia that we should fix it but she said it was the reason she wanted that particular house, so we had left it the way it was. "Baby, dinner is ready!" I heard her call out and rolled my eyes. She called for me as if she'd just finished preparing the meal. I missed Shanice already. Shanice would have cooked an amazing meal for us, but she was just as conservative as they come in the bedroom. Being here with Cecilia, I had to pay a chef to come and prepare every single meal for our family, but I had a woman who'd do anything I asked of her in the bedroom. Most men would say I was living the dream, but all I really wanted was to combine these two women into one. "Okay, I'm coming!" I yelled, throwing on some sweats and a t-shirt because I already knew I'd be rolling around on the floor, playing with Danielle, after dinner. That little girl was everything to me. As much as I told Shanice I didn't want to have kids, I couldn't lie and say I didn't enjoy fatherhood, not to mention looking into a little face that resembled my own so much. Danielle was the best decision I could have ever made, even if it did happen by mistake. I remembered the night she was conceived like it was yesterday, and only because that had been the one and only time that I hadn't used a condom with Cecelia. Our team had a bye week and she'd asked me to come to her family's home for dinner. At first, I was hesitant because she wasn't my girl so there was no reason for me to meet her folks, but she'd promised if I came, I wouldn't regret it. I knew exactly what that meant. I showed up to their beautiful three story home and almost pissed my pants when her dad opened the door, and I was standing face to face with the team owner. "Hey Dandridge, you made it." He didn't seem surprised at all. "Yes sir," I smiled broadly, trying to play it cool but really, I wanted to turn and run the other way. I'd heard stories about guys on the team trying to get close to his daughter and ending up unemployed, so I had no idea why he'd be okay with me. "Cecelia is in the kitchen with her mother. You can join them," he said as he stepped aside, allowing me in. I walked into the kitchen and was greeted by a gorgeous woman who was definitely a direct reflection of Cecelia. Her mother was fine! We started making small talk and that's when Cecelia told me to follow her upstairs because she needed my help hanging a photo she'd just purchased. I had almost declined, considering I'd seen like five different workers since I'd showed up, but I said okay. I followed her into the bedroom and instantly stopped a few feet from the doorway, ready to run. I began to wonder if she was one of those crazy girls with an obsession as I stared at a photograph of my first dunk. I recognized that shot... it had been published when I first joined the team. "Look sweetheart, I don't know what all this is but you're doing a lot. I have a girlfriend, and you're not her." I was trying to be honest. "So you mean to tell me that you have no feelings for me whatsoever?" she challenged. "I love the way it feels to be inside of you," I answered carefully, trying to make her understand, "but that's all, Cecelia." She stepped in close, so close all I had to do was look down to for a personal view of her voluptuous breasts. I watched, mesmerized as her chest rose and fell in short excited breaths as she unbuckled my pants. I wanted to stop her but I had to no willpower. I was a sucker for a woman on her knees. "What if I don't believe you?" she asked as she massaged my dick until it was rock hard. This woman was definitely more direct than Shanice. "You should," I said in a tone that was barely audible. She dropped down to her knees and that's when I noticed she hadn't shut the door. I thought about the possibility of her father catching us but I couldn't move, the feel of my dick in her warm mouth had me in a losing position. I held onto to the back of her head and began to pump myself in and out of her mouth, making sure she was able to feel the tip in her throat. I was expecting her to gag but not one time did Cecelia choke. She started massaging my balls with her hand and from that point, I was a goner. I released my seed down her throat and she stood as if nothing had happened, but now I needed to feel myself inside of her. I ran my hand up the skirt she was wearing and immediately felt her wetness. She'd planned this interlude all along because she wore no panties. I stood at attention more quickly than I thought I would, considering I'd just came not even three minutes before touching her. I lifted her up as she wrapped her legs around my waist and I inserted myself inside of her. All the weight training had paid off because I didn't need anything for stability. I held her hips steady as I thrust myself in and out of her, and hearing her cry out in pleasure made me want to explode. I just knew we were going to get caught. I put her down and told her to get on her knees as I entered her from the doggy style position. I grabbed her hair and rode her like a stallion, and unlike most American women who could barely take me in that position or complained about their weave, she threw it back at me as if we were in competition. "Oh! Oh! Damn girl! Oh, a..." I heard myself cry out like a bitch as I came long and hard. I held onto her while trying to regain myself. Still inside her, I realized I'd just made a mistake, one that I'd never made before, not even with Shanice. I'd not only had sex with her in her parent's home, but I'd just hit this chick raw, and released my seed in her with no regard for what that might do to my future. For the rest of that night, my attitude was more snappy than usual. I prayed our passionate interlude wouldn't become a mistake that cost me everything I'd worked so hard for. Now, here I was... two years later, playing a role in Cecelia's life that I should have been playing in Shanice's.

Chapter 13

SHANICE

heard the doorbell ring and rolled my eyes. Mrs. Harris was two hours late and I knew she'd done it on purpose, making sure there would be something to complain about. The chicken and shrimp Alfredo that I'd made was warming in the oven while I waited, but I was pissed. "Hey," she smiled as she walked in, acting as if she owned the place. "Hello," I greeted her, using my best poker face, "make yourself at home. Shall I take your things?" "What did you cook? I'm starving," she said, ignoring me. Mrs. Harris was trying to act as if she'd been waiting so long to eat. "Well, I made chicken and shrimp Alfredo, with fruit tarts for desert," I told her, proud of my culinary efforts. I'd labored in the kitchen all day preparing the meal so it would be perfect. "Oh no honey, I don't eat no Alfredo nothing," she lied.

Not too long ago, we'd gone to Olive Garden for dinner with Dan, and she'd ordered the exact same meal I prepared for dinner. "Okay well, I guess we can just eat the desert and you can get something else to eat when you leave," I responded, my attitude starting to flare. I was tired of playing nice, just to have her insult me, and be rude to me at every turn. "I really don't even know why I'm here" – "You could have declined," I lashed out, cutting her off before she could make another slick comment. "You're right," she answered, turning on her heel to face the door. "I don't understand why my son sticks around here, to be with you, when he's doing so much better in Spain." She made reference to his life in Spain yet again, and my curiosity finally got the best of me. "Mrs. Harris, if there's something you feel you need to tell me about Dan, just tell me, but don't keep playing these games. Nothing you say can break us, in case you haven't realized that yet," I assured her. "Oh really child... is that's what you think?" Mrs. Harris gleamed, her smile twisted slightly at each corner in a way that made me shiver, but I had to be tough. "It's what I know." I turned to walk away, hoping she'd let herself out. I was not expecting the words she spat at my back. "Well, if you knew so damn much, you'd know that for the past two years, you've been sleeping with a married man." I turned to see the most serious look on her face that I'd ever seen.

Normally, she looked smug, like she just wanted to hurt my feelings but right now, she looked satisfied with airing her son's dirty laundry. "Lies," I spat back at her. "I don't believe it." She was obviously lying, hoping my pain would bring her great pleasure. "Okay sweetie, think I'm lying if you want to! As I told you before, I have a daughter-in-law and a beautiful grandbaby. You're nobody... and I'll be happy when you leave my son the hell alone!" She grabbed her purse and headed toward the door. "That's the main reason I know you're lying to me. All you want is for me to believe you and break things off with Dan! Sorry but your foolishness and lies will never break us," I yelled, standing my ground. I refused to believe that Dan had an entire family in another country when he had refused to give me those things. I wanted the marriage and the kids... there was no way he'd given those things to another woman! No way, I said under my breath.

Chapter 14

MAXWELL

I walked into my mom's house, wondering why the entry way lights were off. She never cut those lights off. She always left them for me to turn off when I got home. I looked around, preparing myself for anything except what I found. "Ma... seriously!" My mother jumped up, knocking over the glass of wine she had sitting in front of her. "I thought you said that you wouldn't be home till late, Maxwell!" "Well, looks like I came home just in time. Who is this nigga feeding you strawberries in the middle of the damn living room?" I wasn't upset that my mother was seeing someone. I was upset that, in all of her prying into my love life, she hadn't mentioned him, and then had the nerve to bring him up in the crib like everybody was cool. "This is Rowland, Max. He's one of the new deacons at the church," she explained. Rowland stood to his feet; he had to be a good 6'5" because he towered over my 6'2" frame. My mom looked like a dwarf standing at 5'4" between us. I guess that would have seemed comical to anyone else. "So this is what y'all do at the deacon board meetings? Hook up and shit?" I accused, still mad. "Wait a minute, son," Rowland started, "I will not have you disrespecting your mother in that way. She's a good wo-" I interrupted him, refusing to allow anyone to call me son. "First of all Rowland, I'm not your son. Second of all you're right. I apologize ma, I just wish you'd given me a heads up that you'd be having company. I could have found something else to do." "Well, why don't you find something now?" Rowland inserted his two cents again and was starting to irk me with his old ass. I had to admit that he was okay looking guy though, moms had done well for herself. He was tall, caramel complexion, hazel eyes, bald head, and nice teeth that looked to be his own. "Aye man, watch yourself! You can't put me out of a house I live in, especially when I know it's because you're trying to get next to my mama. So kiss her goodnight and leave, or you can stay, but I'm joining you two," I chided, deciding to be an asshole. I actually felt like I could grow to like the man. He wasn't no timid dude so I felt my mom was probably in good hands. "Look, young man, I don't want any trouble. I just want to continue enjoying my time with my lady," he gave me a look that said get the hell on. "Alright man, I'm just shocked is all. But give me about 10 minutes, I'll go to Sharon's." My mom started grinning like a Cheshire cat, and I couldn't help but smile. I felt like the parent... this was a weird feeling. "So you must actually like her..." mom mused, taking advantage of the moment to quiz me about my feelings for Sharon again. I shook my head, thinking of how relentless she was when it came to knowing all about my love life. "And you're going to follow my advice?" "Enjoy your date mom." I kissed her cheek and headed up the stairs to call Sharon in private, and to get my overnight bag. Ain't this some shit? I just got put out my own house for some nigga. "I'll meet you at the house," she said curtly. Sharon sounded annoyed that I'd called. She told me she was out having drinks with her friend, Sue. I'd thought that was perfect because I hadn't called her yet about decorating my house, but I could also understand why she'd be upset... considering we didn't have plans. Normally, I wasn't the type to pop up with plans on the fly, but I had no idea my mom would have Rowland over. I pulled up to a beautiful condo and smiled. Sharon was really doing well for herself. I'd been so busy trying to find her flaws that I never really took the time to see that she was actually doing quite well for herself. She pulled up beside me with Sue in the passenger side of her 745 BMW and I was instantly in awe. "Hi, I'm Sue," she purred, reaching out the car window to shake my hand. She kept staring at me, undressing me with her eyes. She was quite a character, I could tell already. "Maxwell," I responded, taking her small hand in mine. She was very attractive, almost as pretty as Sharon, and definitely more experienced, would be my guess. "You sure are handsome," she flirted, continuing to stare. Most females were attracted to my flawless tan skin, pearly whites, and mysterious dark brown eyes. My full lips and body type were a plus. I was definitely a gym rat, which came from being picked on so much in school, because I looked and dressed like Urkel. "Sue, could you not?" Sharon pleaded with her forward friend. I could tell she was a little jealous, but she had no reason to be. I wasn't in the least bit interested in white women. "It's okay," I said, winking at Sharon, "at least somebody compliments me." I shot her a smile to lighten her mood. I didn't want to spend my night with an angry black woman. "Whatever," Sharon giggled, smiling back at me, and I knew I had her. "Sue was just leaving," she added, shooting her a look that let her know this was no threesome. "Damn... okay," Sue sighed, obviously disappointed that she had to leave. "Well Mr. Sexy, call me about that house." She winked and I laughed, not sure which I was enjoying more.... Sue's attention or Sharon's jealous glances. "Mr. Sexy," I smiled broadly as I repeated her words to Sharon, who was shaking her head at her friend. "Yeah, I guess you've just been nicknamed. Well, at least until you mess up and we have to talk about you," she teased. Sharon wore the most beautiful smile and the outfit she had chosen gave a wonderful view of her breasts. I could tell without touching they were the perfect size. "I don't mess up," I challenged her with a smile as I followed her into the building.

Chapter 15

DANDRIDGE

"**C**alm down, baby! Calm down! I can't understand you," I said, raising my voice. Shanice was hysterical and I didn't have much time to talk to her. "Your mother said you have a wife and child in Spain, Dandridge. Can you hear me now?" I couldn't believe she had actually yelled at me! "Stop believing everything my mother tells you! You know she just doesn't want us together," I pleaded with her. I couldn't believe my mom actually told her, and now I had to figure out how to lie my way out of the situation. I'd definitely be having a long talk with La'Draysha Harris. How could she do that? I knew she hated Shanice but it was not her place to tell her my business. "She looked very serious, Dan! If you do, please let me know now," she said, sounding as if she were starting to believe my mother. "Have you been married for two years?" I wanted to go ahead and come clean, but I couldn't. I couldn't let this be the way things ended between me and Shanice. I was quiet for way longer than I needed to be when I heard her speak again. "Damnit, Dan! You are, aren't you?" she accused, in a voice that was suddenly very sad. "No baby, I'm not! And I can't believe you're feeding into my mother's antics. I love you and I'm only with you... nobody else." Her tone softened and I knew she believed me. "Okay Dan," she sighed, even though I couldn't hear the relief in her voice, "but please tell your mother to stop playing games with our relationship. I really just want her to see that I love you and that my being with you has nothing to do with your family's money." "Look baby... I know so that's all that matters," I responded quickly, hearing footsteps coming. "I have to go. I'll call you tomorrow." "Okay, I love you." "I love you too Shanice and nobody else," I said softly into the phone, trying to assure her. She had already hung up the phone, which was odd. I always hung up first. "You're still playing this foolish game," the voice from behind me accused. I turned to find Cecelia standing in the doorway, and I wasn't sure how long she had been there, listening to my conversation. Hopefully, not very long. I'd never lied to her about the situation with Shanice, but I could tell she was starting to get tired of sharing me. "I'm going to end things, Cecilia... I just don't know how." "Looks like you just passed up the perfect opportunity," she responded, glaring at me before turning her back on me and walking away. This was the reason I always tried to talk to Shanice in private. Once again, I was in the doghouse and the only way out was always the same. I'd have to buy yet another expensive gift and whisper sweet nothings so Cecelia would know that I loved her just as much, if not more, than I loved Shanice. This double life was for the birds.

Chapter 16

MAXWELL

I stepped out of the shower with a towel wrapped around my waist and noticed Sharon in the mirror, applying her make-up. I wasn't a fan of sharing the bathroom with anyone because it was a tempting situation but I couldn't put her out of her own bathroom, so I waited till she told me she was dressed before I ended my shower. I'd seen her first thing in the morning, when she had just woken up and she really didn't need the make-up. I never understood why beautiful women felt that they had to be more beautiful by applying make-up while unattractive women, who really needed it, refused to wear the stuff. "You're beautiful without it." Had I said that out loud? She looked up at me as if she were shocked by my comment about her beauty. "Thanks," she countered, "but I'm more confident with it."

"Okay, well there's something wrong with you, then," I began, knowing I should probably remain silent. "Insecurity is unattractive." I could tell she wasn't expecting my honesty but I wasn't the type of guy to hold things back. I'd done that enough times growing up. "Well, everyone can't be as arrogant and overly confident as you!" she quipped, obviously a little annoyed. I could tell that I had offended her. "I'm sorry, Sharon," I apologized. "I'm just being truthful... maybe I'm honest to a fault." "Well, I definitely did not ask for your honesty but thanks for the compliment," she replied with a frown as she looked down into her make-up bag. I was certain that I'd thrown her completely off her task. Turning to leave, I stopped behind her, talking to her reflection in the mirror. "You should wear your hair up. Wearing it down doesn't allow people to really see you." I couldn't believe I had made another comment. This girl was likely going to throw something at me soon. "What are they seeing Maxwell?" she asked, swiveling around in her vanity chair. She looked a little miffed at me still. "You have a beautiful smile, for one. For two, your eyes are mesmerizing and in the right light, they look almost hazel. Your complexion reminds me of brown sugar, pure and flawless. I'm a man but yes, I pay attention." With that statement, I left her to do whatever it was she was going to do with herself. I had no idea why I even cared.

I guess she was growing on me. I called my mom on my way to work to let her know that I'd be moving out of her house very soon. I didn't want to do anything until Sue got finished with the interior decorating. All I had was clothes to move anyway, so it wasn't like I needed her to coordinate the rooms to match any of my belongings. Hell, I need her to choose my furniture too. "Well, I know it's time you get out on your own, son. I don't know why you didn't tell me before," mom admitted. She wasn't upset at all, not that I had really expected her to be. Ma was a strong, black Baptist woman... she could take care of herself. It was the bills that I worried about, knowing she'd be too stubborn to tell me when she needed help. "I know ma, but it's a big move," I warned her. "I bought an entire house." Maybe I had expected her to be a little less supportive. "As long as you're happy in it, son," Ma beamed happily before poking me again. "Maybe you and Sharon will fill it with children." I was getting tired of her being team Sharon. "Yeah maybe," I sighed, deciding not to discuss Shanice, even though she was on my mind. She was always on my mind. Somehow, I was beginning to like Sharon... but I had no idea how that would play out when my love for Shanice was so strong.

Chapter 17

SHANICE

knew it was wrong for me to do what I was doing, but I needed to know the truth. They said curiosity killed the cat but I'd rather the cat die than to be lied to, and I felt like Dandridge was lying to me. I had no idea what I'd do when I got to Spain if it were true... that the man I'd loved since high school was married to another woman and living my dream life with her. I'd made all of my life choices for this man... including a choice that I'd lived to regret till this day. If he'd betrayed me like this I'd kill him. My phone rang just as they'd called my boarding zone and something told me not to answer, but I didn't need to raise any suspicion. "Hello?" I said innocently. "Hey baby, what are you doing?" he asked, sounding happy to hear my voice. I immediately got angry hearing his. "Nothing," I answered, just as they announced the next zone. "Are you in the airport?" he questioned, sounding more than a little concerned, but I would put his mind at ease. "Yeah, just dropped Tameka off," I lied. "I thought you guys weren't talking?" he tried me. "She's my sister, Dan. How long did you think that would last?" I was on point with my responses. I didn't need him questioning me any further. "Okay, okay... sorry," he stammered before quickly recovering. "I was just calling to say I love you but your energy is all off, so I guess I'll let you say bye to your sister." "Umm-hmm, love you too," I answered as I hung up on him. I couldn't wait till my plane landed in Spain because if that nigga was found anywhere but the apartment address he'd given me, there would be big problems.

Chapter 18

DANDRIDGE

I walked into the house with flowers and a new tennis bracelet for Cecelia. I had no idea what else to buy a woman who had everything, but I was damn sure going to try impressing her, as best I could. She'd banished me from her bedroom to our hard ass couch for three days now and it was killing my back. I just wanted to be next to my wife, but I also had a sneaking suspicion that Shanice was lying to me, and she'd hopped a plane to Spain. I'd have to come up with a reason to stay a few nights at my apartment to save face. Shanice only had one address for me in Spain and it wouldn't help my case at all if I wasn't there when she landed. My mom had been ignoring my calls because she knew I was upset with her, but we'd talk eventually. She wasn't going to ignore my calls forever. I decided to give Max a call to see if he knew what was up. "Hey, man!" I crooned into the phone, happy to hear my boy's voice. He'd help a nigga out. "You can't call nobody?" "Man, I've been busy... been dating a little and working a lot," he answered, but it seemed like the last thing he wanted to do was hear from his boy. I needed his help so I pretended not to notice. "You seen Shannie, man?" I called Shanice by her nickname, instantly realizing that was something I normally wouldn't do. Oh well, it was too late now... best to just go with it. "No, why?" Max answered, sounding a little offended that I'd asked. "I think she's on her way here but I don't know for sure. You think you can talk to my mom for me? She's ignoring my calls," I asked, trying to get him to do me a solid without giving him too much information. I had no idea what was going on between me and him, but I knew he was acting different. "Why is your mom ignoring you?" This dude was asking too many questions. "You know what, bruh? Don't worry about it," I said, hiding my disdain. "I'll just keep calling." I wasn't about to get into this conversation with him. I didn't know who the hell he thought he was giving me the third degree, but I wasn't on it. Cecelia and Danielle walked in the house and Danielle jumped on me before I knew it. She was always so happy to see me and I loved it. "Look at what I got," she beamed proudly, showing me her new American Doll, and I only shook my head at her mother. I never understood why people paid so much for dolls when the kids were only going to mistreat them. It wasn't like she was old enough to know to take care of it. "She's beautiful, just like you baby girl," I told her and she lit up like a Christmas tree. "And these are for you," I added, handing Cecelia the flowers and jewelry box. She took them both and threw them on the counter as if I hadn't given her a thing. "That's not working this time, Dan. I've given you two years to get rid of this American slut and you refuse. You break it off soon or I'm leaving and you'll never see your daughter again." I hated when she used our child as leverage. "I will, Cecelia," I sighed, counting the times I'd asked her not to call Shanice names. Tonight wasn't the night to mention it, though. "That's what you've said since we married. I don't believe you. You stay on the couch until it's done," she warned me before storming upstairs, leaving me to play with Danielle. That was alright though, because I'd already made up in my mind that, after I put my daughter to bed, I'd write her a note and go to the apartment.

Chapter 19

MAXWELL

"You look nice," I complimented Sharon. I'd been at her house for close to a week. My mom seemed to invite Rowland to the house every night of the week, now that her secret was out, and I wasn't trying to be the third wheel to two old folks who were, as they called it, courting. "Thanks," she smiled. She was wearing a simple black spaghetti strap dress with a pair of red heels, and I could tell that my opinion mattered to her, because she had her hair up in a neat bun and wore no make-up, other than eye shadow. I figured I'd take her out to dinner since she'd been the perfect host, and hadn't complained once about me being there longer than a night. We'd talked a lot and I learned that she graduated top of her class in high school, and college too. Her original plan was to attend to law school but decided against it, stating that she was just tired of school, which I didn't understand, considering I was about to get my master's in less than a month. In this time, I had also learned that she had a very close relationship with her mother and three sisters. Their dad, like mine, had left their mom to start another family and never looked back, so she had four siblings on his side of the family but she'd never established a relationship with them. "I see you took my advice," I smiled sheepishly. "Sorry if I offended you for being so forward that day. I never apologized." "It's okay. It just took me by surprise most men aren't as honest, or forward as you", she admitted with a small smile. "It's a great character trait. At least then I know there are no games." She looked down as if she were nervous to talk to me. "Something on your mind?" I asked, mentally trying to decide what was eating at her. I could tell by the look on her face that she was perplexed. "Well, I was just wondering, and I don't want you to take this the wrong way …or for this to ruin your opinion of me, but why haven't you tried anything with me?" she asked quietly, as if embarrassed to bring it up even though her question had obviously been eating at her. "Not even so much as a kiss?" I could tell the question stemmed from a concern rather than a need for casual sex. I was a good judge of character and Sharon wasn't that kind of girl, anyway.

"How about this? Let's head to dinner and by the end of the night, I will make sure you have your answer." I knew that, if we stayed in the house, I'd kiss her just because I knew she wanted to me to, and I'd probably end up making love to her because there had been many times this week that I wanted to, but she wasn't my girlfriend and I didn't need sex complicating what we were building.

Chapter 20

SHANICE

I was approaching my fourth day in Spain and nothing seemed odd or different between me and Dandridge. He'd go to practice and come straight home, and took me out every night. He'd take me to different places in different cities because he said there wasn't much to do in the city where he lived. The only thing I didn't like was his refusal when I asked to sit in on his practices. I hadn't seen him play outside of the DVD's he'd send back home since high school, and I hated feeling like that part of his life was his alone. "So, how long do I have with you?" he questioned me, trying to drown me in his charm. "You show up... you surprise me, but you still haven't told me how long you're staying?" "I leave at the end of the month," I finally told him. I didn't know why it mattered really, and I was praying that he wasn't asking because he had some other woman to accommodate, but after the past few days, I felt like the other woman would have to be stupid to not wonder where he was spending his days and nights. Still, I hadn't ruled out the possibility of her existence. "Okay well, that means I only have a month to do this." He kissed me and leaned me back on the bed. He ran his hand up my thigh and began to massaging my love until his fingers were completely wet. He brought his fingers to his lips and licked me off, one finger at a time, as he looked straight into my eyes. I wanted him so bad, I almost begged for it, but I wanted to see what he was going to do next. Dan always liked being in control of our sex. He pulled me to the edge of the bed and dropped to his knees in front of me. I knew what he was about to try, and I stopped him. "Baby, you know I don't like that." "Shannie, how can you not like what you've never let me try?" he pleaded. It was the same argument as last time. It hadn't worked then either. "Can we just do it how we always do?" I asked sweetly, trying to salvage the moment. "Ok." I could tell it was too late. I'd already messed up the mood for him, but he knew I didn't want him going down on me. I just felt that it was so nasty to put your mouth on someone's private parts. He dropped his pants and gave me an apologetic look. He wasn't hard. "I guess I turned you off," I admitted. Even though I was a bit hurt, I also understood. "Yeah, you did," he answered and I could tell he was pissed. "Well, maybe I can jack you off and we'll be able to get him interested again." I tried to keep a positive attitude. "No, I'm good, man," he answered coldly, dismissing me with complete indifference. I watched as he got dressed without uttering another word, until he headed for the door. "Where are you going, Dan?" "Don't worry about it," he snapped, before deciding his answer had been a little too harsh. "I'll be back a little later. I just can't be in here with you right now." I knew how much he desired for us to have oral sex, but I just couldn't do it. I wanted him to understand that I just wasn't that type of girl, but I guess he never would. I threw on some jeans and decided I'd follow him. I wanted to make sure he wasn't going to get his needs met elsewhere, because Dan never left me without telling me where he was going.

Chapter 21

DANDRIDGE

I got in my car and headed home. I'd been going home and spending the day with my daughter every day since Shanice had shown up by telling her I was going to practice. I didn't care what decisions I made. As long as I was around, I was going to make sure I was an active father. But this trip home was different, it was late, and if Shanice wasn't willing to give me what I wanted, I knew Cecelia would... regardless of her being upset. The one thing that woman would never turned down was sex. With each turn of my steering wheel, I had an uneasy feeling... a feeling that, if I didn't come clean with Shanice before she left Spain, things would blow up in my face. Maybe it was a good thing that she was lacking sexually because that was a very big deal for me. As I turned into my driveway I set a reminder in my phone to tell Shanice it was over... first thing tomorrow. I walked into the house and tiptoed up the steps. Cecelia was the type of woman who liked to wake up with your tongue between her legs. In her opinion, nothing compared to the feeling, not even her morning coffee. I remembered the first time I'd done it. She put her hands on the back of my head and pushed me so deep into her ocean, I just knew I'd drown. I smiled at the thought. The door to the bedroom was ajar and Cecelia looked so lovely sleeping, as the light from the window provided just enough light for me to enjoy her beauty. I stepped inside the room and undressed at the door, careful not to make any noise. I loved that she always slept naked; I don't think I'd had a Spanish woman yet who didn't. I had no idea how Maxwell never dealt with Mexican women, considering he was half Mexican. I felt Spanish was Spanish; if you speak it, you're it. A lot of people called me ignorant for thinking that way, but I didn't care. I peeled back the cover, just enough to expose her as I took in her body. My wife was beautiful. I was blessed to have had two beautiful women loving me at the same time. I gently moved her so that she'd be on her back. She started to stir a little but didn't wake. I spread her legs just as gently, and began to feast until I felt her hands on my head like she normally did whenever I did this. I stuck my tongue as deep as I could and ate her like she was the only woman in the world. I worked my way up to her clit and began to roll my tongue on it as she moved her hips to my rhythm, she began to moan softly, then a little louder until I knew she was nearing her orgasm. I'd learned that, when a woman was about to come, you don't move. You stay in that spot until she rides that wave or you'll mess up what you worked so hard for her to get. Her body gave way to the orgasm and I was ready to feel myself buried deep inside of her warmth. I hadn't made love to her in so long, I prayed I wouldn't tap out too fast. I entered her and began moving slowly, careful not to do too much too soon. I pulled her close to me so that we'd be body to body. She started kissing and biting my neck, just like she knew I liked. I picked up the pace and pounded myself into her and each cry of ecstasy that escaped her lips let me know that I was making the right choice. I loved Shannie but I needed my wife... needed her like I'd never needed anyone. I turned us over so Cecelia could ride me, and so I could look straight up into her eyes. I grabbed ahold of her hips as she grinded her clit on my dick hard and reached her climax. She turned around in reverse cowgirl and I smacked her ass while loving the show. She stretched herself out in what seemed like the push up position and continued her mission. I could no longer hold on. I released my hot seed all in her and held her for the rest of the night. I prayed that God would forgive me for the way I'd mistreated and handled both women, but tomorrow I'd be a new man, a man who was faithful to his wife.

Chapter 22

MAXWELL

I stood before all of my peers, my mom, Rowland and Sharon, wearing a smile. Today was the day that I got promoted from 2nd lieutenant to Captain. I never thought I'd be living this day out without having Shanice there for support, even if Dan was with her, but from what I'd been told, she was visiting him in Spain. My mother loved herself some Sharon, so she was glad that it was Sharon by my side instead of Shanice. As much as loved me and thought Shanice was a good person, she felt I needed to move on and be with someone who actually noticed me, and Sharon did just that. She'd started taking a page out of my book ...so to speak, being blunt and honest about the things she liked and didn't like when it came to me. She hated that I never really dressed up or looked like I was going out. I loved

80

sneakers so I always had on nice shoes, but it was either with a pair of black or grey sweatpants and a shirt to match the shoes. Or, if we went out to eat, I'd wear a nice pair of Levi's instead. I was a simple man, whom Sharon was trying to turn into a complicated one. I hated shopping outside of footlocker. "I just want to thank God first because without him, I wouldn't be here, and I definitely wouldn't have made it through two consecutive deployments. I also want to thank my mother, who raised me to be the man I am, and teaching me to go for my goals …no matter what they were. She raised me to be an upstanding adult. I'd like to thank the unit for entrusting me with such a title. I will aim to be the best commander this unit has seen." During my speech, I saw Sharon look down. I don't know if she was expecting a thank you but I hoped she wasn't, considering she'd only been around a little over a month and I'd only been at her house for a couple of weeks. I loved the time I'd spent with her, but I was ready for Sue to finish decorating my house so I could officially move. I'd seen it in its unfinished state, and I could instantly tell that she was great at what she did. It was the perfect mixture of masculinity but with a woman's touch. I felt that no woman would want to come in and change a thing, because it had the perfect balance. She'd told me it would be finished next week and that was great news to me. We finished up at my company and I decided to take Sharon and my mom to dinner. Sharon had been looking at her feet ever since I gave my speech, so I figured I'd talk to her in the car on the way to Applebee's. My mom chose to ride with Rowland, so we'd have enough time to talk privately. "What's up?" I asked. "Why've you been looking so sad?" "I don't know. I expected some kind of acknowledgement I guess," she admitted, letting me know that I was right. "I just felt a little left out," she added. "Acknowledgement for what exactly, Sharon?" I asked, hoping her response would cure any confusion. "Nothing," she sighed, looking out the window. "Let's just forget it." I could tell she didn't want to express herself but I needed her to be honest with me about her feelings. "No, please tell me," I asked her again. I hoped she would give me a reason that wasn't at all petty or childish, but that was probably too much to expect. "Just for being your friend and showing up, I guess," she cantered, choosing her words cautiously. "You explained the other night that you hadn't touched me because we're not together. We're building from our friendship and I get that, but I didn't have to take the time off to support you. I wanted to, so you'd know I'm there when you need me. But I couldn't even get a thank you for coming to support you ...and on such a big day for your career." She looked at me and I could tell it hurt her feelings a little.

Sharon was pretty sensitive and that was okay with me, because I hated women who felt they always had to be hard about everything… or felt that showing emotion to a man meant she was showing him he could run over her and hurt her. "I apologize, Sharon. I really didn't think about it. But I do appreciate you coming and supporting me; thank you." "You're welcome," she responded sweetly. With that, I took her hand in mine and held it for the rest of the drive to Applebee's. Sharon was slowly finding a place in my heart and in my life.

Chapter 23

SHANICE

paid the driver for following Dan and stepped out of the taxi, pausing to stand outside this gorgeous home. I watched from across the street as he slid his key into the lock, so I knew that this was either his home or someone he was very close to. I decided that I'd wait awhile, just to see how long he stayed. After about three hours of waiting, I realized he wasn't going to come out. I dialed his cell number and it went straight to voicemail so I knew he had to be with a woman. Dan had a habit of cutting his phone off at bedtime. We'd had more than a few incidents of females calling him at all times of night, so he felt it would just be better if he cut his phone off to keep down arguments and, even though it sounded stupid, it worked for us. Tonight, knowing that he'd walked in this house and done the same thing he normally does with me let me know that I was on the right track to finding out what was going on with Dan and our relationship. I decided to start walking until I found another taxi. I rode back to the hotel with a plan to return to that house, first thing in the morning. Hopefully, Dan would still be there and I'd get the answers I needed. I called my sister, Tameka, whom I hadn't spoken to in months. We'd gotten into an argument because our drug addicted mother came to her, asking for over two thousand dollars, and when she called me, I refused to ask Dan for it or go into my savings and get what I could. I was tired of enabling her. She'd been on drugs since I was in the eighth grade, so my grandmother took custody of me and my younger sister, and raised us as best she could. My sister hadn't really done much with her life, outside of having kids with three different deadbeats and becoming the manager at Burger King. She did what she could for her kids but most times, it came down to me and my grandmother loaning her money that we would never get back. "Oh, so you know my number?" she asked coyly, with a lot of attitude. "Look Meka," I sighed. "I don't want to go through this right now. I really don't have the energy." My emotions were running too high to play cat and mouse with her today. "What's wrong, big sis?" she asked, sensing the sadness in my voice. "I think Dan is cheating on me," I began, but before I could continue with any details, she cut me off. "So, what's new about that? Oh, please don't tell me you're chasing that nigga around Spain." "Never mind," I said with a sigh, "I don't even know why I called." "No," Tameka responded, coaxing me to stay on the line with a soft crooning voice, "it's cool. But you know I always felt like you should be with his friend Maxwell anyway. That man is fine and you know he's always liked you. He used to follow you and Dan around like a puppy. I think it was just to be close to you." I thought my sister sounded delusional... because there was no way Max liked me or even thought of me in that way. I had to laugh though because, growing up, Max was like a half Mexican and black Steve Urkle. He wore the suspenders and glasses with string to keep them on his face. He was really smart though, and I just knew he was going to marry Kimberly Hill. Kimberly Hill... I hadn't heard or thought of that name for a long time. She was the girl who'd broken his heart on his first deployment by sleeping with one of his soldiers that stayed back in the rear. Max had given that girl everything she wanted. He had been so gullible when it came to her. I hadn't seen him with anyone since, but I knew he wasn't secretly pining for me. "I did not call for you to go on and on about how you think Max wants me. Thank you very much," I replied, more than a little annoyed. "Why can't you just be helpful and supportive like normal sisters?" I knew calling her wasn't a good idea but I'd needed someone to talk to so badly. "Well, you need to listen because Dan ain't got nothing on Max. I mean Dan is fine and all, but Maxwell is so fine that I'd give it to him ...even if he dated my mama first," she giggled, sounding like his biggest fan. "Well if you think he's so fine, why don't you try to get with him?" I asked. "Because he doesn't like me," Tameka explained, "I wish he did, though." I laughed at how pressed my sister was for Max. "Okay look, sis. When I get back home, I'll put in a good word for you. You're beautiful, Meka. I know he'll go out with you," I replied, shaking my head. Meka never ceased to amaze me. "If you say so, big sis," she said, laughing. "I won't be mad if he confesses his undying love for you though." Tameka was in such a good mood and saying such silly things, I found myself smiling again too, but I was also feeling tired. "He won't," I responded, sure that she was completely wrong in her assumptions. "But hey... I'm about to go to bed. I have an interesting morning planned. I love you, Meka." "I love you too," she sighed, her voice sounding far more serious now. "Stay safe out there with Dan's trifling, cheating ass." As I hung up the phone, I realized that I'd just talked to my sister about everything except what I'd called her for, and the funny thing was, the conversation had improved my mood. I just hoped that all went well tomorrow with Dan, and that Max would agree to take my sister out.

Chapter 24

DANDRIDGE

"Good morning baby," I whispered to Cecelia as I felt her moving to get out of bed. "Just because you slept here last night, that doesn't mean we've made up, Dandridge." She spoke to me coldly and I'm sure it didn't help that I laughed. "How long do you really want to be mad?" I knew she couldn't stay mad at me forever, especially after I'd been so good to her last night. "As long as it takes you to leave her alone, Dan," she warned. "Okay, well what if I told you that I'm going to take you and Danny to breakfast, and right after that, I'm going to end things?" I asked, hoping to break through the shell she was trying to build around herself. "She's in town... you can even go with me." I saw the biggest smile form across her lips. "And I won't have to share you anymore?" Cecelia beamed. "No, Mrs. Harris I'm all yours," I promised. She jumped into my arms and kissed me more passionately than she ever had. Had it not been for the sound of small footsteps, I was sure we would have continued our rendezvous from last night. "Go ahead, get her ready, and by the time you two are done, I'll be downstairs waiting." I kissed her softly and headed to the shower. I waited downstairs for my two favorite girls to get ready for breakfast. I started going through my phone, deleting all traces of Shanice, when I came across my favorite picture of us. She'd dabbled in photography during our junior year of college and decided to set her camera up on a tripod to take some intimate photos of the two of us. In this particular photo, I literally had my finger inside of her and her head was tilted back on my shoulder, my free arm covering her breasts. I didn't understand how she could be so free in front of the camera that day, but never so free in the bedroom. It really blew me. I took one last look at the picture before deleting it. Without even reading through our text messages, I deleted them all. This was one of the steps I needed to take to get her out of my system, though I knew she'd never completely leave my heart and mind. The hardest thing I'd ever have to do would be breaking her heart completely. She'd made so many sacrifices for me, and there was one sacrifice she could never take back, and I knew it bothered her every day. I felt like a monster. "We're ready," Cecilia chimed, taking me away from my thoughts. Smiling her brightest, prettiest smile, I knew she'd waited for this day so long. "Let's go then," I replied, jumping off of the couch to grab my keys. My daughter reached up for me to carry her as we headed for the door. She loved being in my arms and I loved having her there. She was my pride and joy.

Chapter 25

MAXWELL

"I respect your opinion on a lot of things, Max... but you don't live here! You can't control when my friends come over," Sharon argued. "I'm not trying to control when they come over," I replied calmly, trying to explain. "I'm just saying that, while I'm here, it's not cool for your friends to just come and go as they please ...just because they have a key." "It's not like we're doing anything," she sighed, rolling her eyes and walking away, obviously frustrated. I'd never seen a woman so pressed for a guy to touch her. I felt that would be an ongoing issue for the two of us. How could she not understand that I was waiting on the woman God had for me? I was a smart guy and I knew that STD's and babies happened, so I wasn't down to let it happen to me. I didn't want to be treated for being stupid, and I didn't want kids with a woman I wasn't going to spend the rest of my life with. If my situation growing up hadn't shown me anything else, it taught me that I wanted to be settled in my career and with my wife before we started popping out babies. "Look. I get that you want to feel wanted," I said, trying to reason with her after a few minutes had passed, "but I'm here, right?" "Yes," she replied, speaking a little more softly than she had before. I knew Sharon was a little jaded from past relationships, and didn't know how to react to a man that wasn't out for sex. "Okay... well, chill. All I'm asking is that, for the next few days when Sue comes over, she doesn't use her key. We were relaxing comfortably, watching a movie, and in she walks disturbing that," I explained. "She came over to let you know your place would be finished Sunday," she repeated. Sharon still didn't understand. "Sharon. I have a phone... do I not?" I said, trying to explain again. I could tell she felt stupid for even going there with me, but I continued. "Just as easily as she came over here sticking her key in that lock, she could have picked up her phone and called. When I'm spending time with someone I hate interruptions, especially surprise interruptions." I saw a smile starting to form on her face. "If I didn't know any better, Mr. Taylor, I'd say you liked me," she gleamed, wrapping her arms around my waist. I responded, quickly embracing her. "You're okay," I laughed, kissing her on the forehead. "Now can we please get back to this movie? I still can't believe you haven't seen Love and Basketball." I shook my head for emphasis. "I was never a big movie girl," she shrugged, shuffling her feet across the floor playfully as she followed me back into the living room. My phone rang more times than I could count while Sharon lay against my chest on the couch. We'd spent our entire day watching movies she hadn't seen, falling asleep when she decided to make me watch The Notebook. I was down for a chick flick but that movie was just too damn long for me. I reached down to grab my phone, slipping it out of my shoe. My heart nearly stopped when I realized that over a dozen missed calls were from Shanice. I wanted to call her back but I didn't want to disrespect Sharon. I was letting Shanice go, and I had no idea why she'd be calling me anyway. I hadn't heard from Dan since the night he got upset because I wouldn't insert myself into his business without knowing the situation. And after the awesome night I'd had with Sharon, as much as my heart longed for Shanice, I was in no mood to hear about her and Dan's problems.

Chapter 26

SHANICE

Dan opened the front door right as I pressed the doorbell, and my heart almost dropped to my feet. "Shanice," he gasped, under his breath. He sounded shocked as I took in the scene before me. "Daddy let's go, let's go," pleaded the little girl in his arms. She seemed to know him well. The moment felt so surreal... as if I were in some sort of trance. Before I truly realized what was going on, he put the little girl down and I could see the apology in his eyes. "Well, no time like the present," the woman standing behind him crooned. "We'll be inside, baby." The beautiful woman took the girl from his arms and led her back inside. The little one wasn't happy with being taken from her daddy's arms, and was even less amused that their trip had been postponed. They were both beautiful and the little girl was a direct reflection of Dan. With tears in my eyes, I'd slapped him before I knew it and turned to walk away. "Shanice, wait! Wait!" I heard him yelling after me but my feet kept moving. "Shanice!" He caught up to me and grabbed my arm. "You sorry bastard!" I yelled, twisting my shoulder to break his grip on my arm. "Don't you ever touch me!" "Ok, I deserved that," Dan admitted, "but how'd you find me?" "How'd I find you? That's all you have to say to me? After eleven fucking years, all you have to say is how did I find you?" I asked, more upset than I'd ever been. "I followed your trifling ass last night!" I told him the truth. "I can't believe you followed me," he said, avoiding the questions I'd asked. Dan was still trying to play his head games. "You know what, Dandridge? Just stop! Why did you waste my time like this? Made your mother out to be a liar but clearly, you just didn't have the balls to tell me the truth." I couldn't even look at him the same. He stood there looking at me like he didn't even care. "Well, you know now," he shrugged, acting as if everything I'd just said to him meant nothing. "I have a wife and a little girl." I started hitting him, swinging blindly as my cries became hysterical. "How could you do this to me? You gave her everything I ever wanted! I had an abortion just to make your ass happy and here you are being daddy to another bitch child!" "Don't call her bitch," he said in a low voice, warning me. "She's not that at all. She's my wife, Shanice." Those words cut me deeper than any knife ever could. Not only had he betrayed me, but he defended her in a way that he never had with me. "What did I do to deserve this, Dan?" I asked numbly, no longer caring what he had to say. I'd been living a lie all this time. "You didn't do anything. You're a real great woman and you deserve someone better than me," Dan said, taking a deep breath before continuing, "And hopefully that man can get you to open up sexually because in eleven years, God knows I couldn't." He turned to walk away, and as he disappeared into his family's home, I was left standing there with my tears. I had no idea how I'd get through this one. I'd given up so much for him. I'd aborted my child because he didn't want kids, and now I was left with nothing. I went to the hotel and packed my things. I called Maxwell over a dozen times and he hadn't answered. It wasn't like him. Why wasn't he accepting my calls? I didn't really know who else I could talk to. I thought maybe Max could help me understand what happened, considering they were best friends... almost like brothers. That's when it dawned on me that Max probably knew all about Dan's secret life, and the realization left me feeling betrayed by two men. Maybe Dan had already gotten to him and Max would cut me off too. I had no idea what anyone was thinking at this point. I just knew that, in a matter of minutes, my whole life had changed and I wasn't sure if it was for the better.

Chapter 27

DANDRIDGE

It broke my heart, having to be so cold toward Shanice, but I knew that if I'd allowed myself to show any type of compassion for her and her tears, the only thing I would have wanted was to be with her ...to make things right. She would never know how much I loved her, but I needed to start making moves for my family. Cecelia and Danielle were the only two women that mattered, and I had a lot of making up to do when it came to the both of them. "So I guess we're not going to breakfast?" Cecelia's voice brought me back to reality. I was relieved to escape my thoughts, and what I had done to the girl I'd basically grown up with. "Yes, we're going," I promised her, flashing the best smile I could muster. "I'm sorry, baby," she apologized. I really didn't understand why she was telling me that, after all I had put her through. "For what?" Curiosity got the best of me. I wanted to know what she was thinking. "I know it's hard, losing someone you care about. I'm sorry for the hard time I gave you. I know she meant something to you, but I promise you won't regret choosing us," she answered softly as she leaned in close to me, looking very sincere. "I should have chosen you two long ago," I answered truthfully. "There's no need for you to apologize. I should be the one apologizing. I love you, Cecelia." I pulled her into my arms and a single tear fell from my eye. It would be the only tear I shed for Shanice because it was time for both of us to move forward. I spent the rest of the day doing whatever Cecelia wanted to do, and the more I tried to focus on her and Danny, the harder it was. I wondered what Shanice was going to do... if she'd keep the condo or move out, if she'd have any contact with my family or if they'd contact her. My mother hated her but my sisters loved her. They never agreed with the way I handled this situation. I had to get in touch with her in a few days, just to make sure she was okay.

Chapter 28

MAXWELL

"**G**irl, I told you my church was the truth!" I beamed, excited that Sharon had agreed to go to church with me. I'd just moved all my clothes into the house, with her help, while my mom cooked dinner in my kitchen. She just couldn't resist. "I admit it was a great service, but the crazy thing was you being in the choir," she laughed. Sharon had no idea that I was a man of many talents and one of them was being able to sing my ass off. A lot of people had compared my voice to the late Jerald Levert, but I never really took that to heart. "What's so funny about it? Lots of singers are guys," I responded, challenging her. "Nothing is actually funny," she chimed playfully. "I was just surprised to hear such a voice come out of you is all." "Girl, I'm an all-around kind of man," I promised, smiling at her. I couldn't help but stare into her eyes. She was so pretty. "I see that," Sharon agreed, "how'd I get so lucky?" Her question threw me off. Sharon and I had spent a lot of time together, and I knew the talk about us was eventually going to come up. I just didn't want to have it while my mother and Rowland were around. "I don't know," I whispered, winking at her, "but we'll discuss it after dinner." I felt that I was ready to tell Sharon what she wanted to hear. She was an amazing woman and I'd have to be a fool to let her go based on the assumption that one day Shanice might want me. Sharon and I enjoyed dinner with my mom and Rowland. We all kicked back and laughed at old stories my mom and Rowland both told about life. To hear Rowland tell it, he was a real gangsta back his day. I could tell he made my mother happy. All and all, I was happy for both of them. "Well, you two lovebirds, it's getting late," mom began, "we're going to get going. You haven't gotten your cable installed, and lifetime is airing a new movie tonight." Everyone in the room laughed, knowing how my mother loved her lifetime. "Okay, y'all have a good night. I love you, ma." I walked the two of them to the door. Rowland was even growing on me, I thought, shaking his hand. "We will. I love you too and I'm proud of you son. Keep Sharon around. She's a real sweet woman," my mom said, whispering in a voice that everyone could hear. She kissed me on the cheek while Rowland held the door. "So, what do you want to do now?" Sharon asked as I closed the door behind them. "You can help me with the dishes," I teased, unfastening my Gucci watch and laying it on the sofa table. "Help... or do them? Every time you asked for help at my house, I ended up doing them," she stated, giving me a look. "No, I'm going to help for real this time. You wash, I'll dry," I promised. We went into the kitchen and I pulled her into my arms for a long kiss. "What was that for?" she asked. "Just because," I said softly, looking deep into her eyes. I could see how much she longed for me. "What are we doing, Max?" she asked. "We're...," I began, but my answer was interrupted by the sound of my doorbell ringing excessively.

Chapter 29

SHANICE

I rang Maxwell's doorbell over and over again. I had no idea if he'd moved into the house yet, but his car was outside and it was the last place Dan told me about. He was excited for Max, telling me that he'd bought his first home, and apparently his future families home. I had no idea Max was doing so well for himself but as his friend, I had been very proud of him. Max swung the door open, looking upset. "Shanice!" he exclaimed, sounding surprised. I watched as his whole demeanor changed. "I'm sorry to just drop by your house, but I really needed someone to talk to." I was on the verge of tears just mentioning the fact that I needed to talk. I was so consumed with the fact that I needed him that I barely noticed the very pretty brown skinned girl standing behind him. "Sharon," he said, introducing us, "this is Shanice. Shanice, Sharon." He didn't seem upset that I'd called on him, but I still felt bad interrupting them. "I'm sorry if you were busy, Maxwell," I said, trying to excuse myself. "I can come back later." "No. Come in," he said, stepping aside to let me in. As I entered the foyer and looked around the room, I could instantly see why Max had chosen this house. It was absolutely stunning. "Just give me a minute. The living room is right through there." He pointed in the direction of the living room area. I hated to interrupt his date, but I didn't feel it could be too important if he let me in anyway.

Chapter 30

MAXWELL

Sharon looked like she wanted to slap me into next week once Shanice was out of sight. "Look Sharon, I know we were in the middle of a talk, but Shanice is one of my really good friends and she needs me right now," I explained, but she wasn't as understanding as I thought she should be. "You're in love with her, Maxwell!" Sharon said in a whisper, her eyes full of anger. "Excuse me?" I asked, feigning shock and surprise. I didn't think it was that obvious and now, I wasn't sure which would be worse... telling her the truth or acting as if I were being unjustly accused. "Maxwell, the way your eyes followed her, and the way your demeanor changed when you noticed who was at the door said it all." It wasn't jealousy and I didn't have the heart to accuse her. "Sharon, I'm sorry," I began, before she cut me off. "Don't," she ordered firmly. "Just do me a favor. Don't use her like you've clearly used me." Her eyes glistened with anger and I could tell she was on the verge of tears. It killed me to know that I'd hurt someone because that was never my intention. And now, I was torn, hating to turn my back on Sharon, but every second that passed while Shanice waited in the next room was more than I could bear. I walked into the living room and Shanice threw herself into my arms before saying a word. "What's wrong?" I asked, although I had a pretty good idea. "Please tell me you didn't know, Max," she sniffled, stepping back so she could look into my eyes. Her eyes were filled with tears, and I knew she'd finally found out the truth about Dan. I didn't want to lie to her, but I also feared the truth would send her running to someone else. I couldn't answer because I didn't want to be another Dan in her life, but I also didn't want to lose Shanice before I ever got the chance to tell her I loved her. "Max?" "Yeah, Shanice, I knew," I answered honestly. "So everybody knew except me? I must be the dumbest bitch ever!" With determination to stop crying, she wiped the tears away from her cheeks with her hands, and I could see anger replacing the hurt in her eyes. "It wasn't my place to tell you," I admitted, hating the position that Dandridge had put me in with Shanice.

"Well I wish someone had." "You can do better, Shanice. Trust me. I've barely spoken to Dan myself since I found out," I told her, hoping she'd take a second look at the man standing in front of her. She seemed happy to hear that someone might be on her side. "I just can't believe he did this to me, Max," she mumbled sadly, "Eleven years of my life, wasted." "Did you learn from it?" I asked, trying to give her a little bit of hope that someday, this would be a lesson in the rear view... that she'd take something good from this whole experience. "I guess," she shrugged, and I knew she hadn't really processed what had taken place. She hadn't reached that pivotal point to know if she'd learned from Dan's tomfoolery or not. In that moment, I promised myself I wouldn't make any moves before I knew she was truly over him. "How about you stay here with me for a little while? I'll take some time off work and we can just hangout," I explained. "It might help you take your mind off Dan." I knew it would be less painful here than in the penthouse, where everything would remind her of him. "Sounds like a plan," she sighed with a smile. It was the first smile I'd seen since she rang the doorbell, and it made me feel better too. "But Max? There's one thing." "What?" "My sister is very interested in you," she began, "I pro..." "No, Shanice," I interrupted, not wanting to hear the rest. "I'm okay! Your sister is a beautiful girl and all, but I'm really not interested,"

I shut down that conversation before it even got started. I was on a mission to make Shanice mine... not Tameka.

Chapter 31

DANDRIDGE

It had been a little over a week since Shanice left me and my heart ached like no pain I could have ever imagined. Cecelia was already getting on my nerves, and so was my mother. She'd called me over a dozen times with her fake apology for telling Shanice about Cecelia and Danny, and I wasn't buying it, but she was my mother so I had to forgive her. I decided I'd give my dad a call. If anybody knew about the drama of letting go of a double life, he did. "Hey son, it's been a while," he answered, sounding happy to hear from me. Even though he was my dad, I couldn't help but feel intrusive when I heard voices in the background. "You busy, dad?" I wasn't sure if he was actually pleased that I had called. I'd give him a chance to excuse himself. "Never too busy for my children," he answered, "you know that.

What's going on?" Relieved that he had time, I took a deep breath and began. "I lost Shanice. I was planning to end things, but the way it happened made me look like I never really loved her at all, and I really do." I wanted to breakdown in tears just expressing my feelings to dad. "Sometimes, marrying for children isn't the right move, son. You have to be happy," he explained. "Are you happy?" "No," I admitted. I'd been so consumed with my own selfish thoughts that I'd let go of the best woman for me because her needs and desires weren't important to me. Shanice had given up the life she wanted so desperately for me, and I couldn't make the sacrifices she needed me to make.

10 years prior

"You the man, boy!" My teammates gave me props for an outstanding practice. I was the best thing on Forrest Hill Preps varsity basketball team, and I was only a sophomore. I felt like my life was perfect. I had the finest girl in school, Shanice Fuller. My grades were on point, thanks to my super smart best friend, Maxwell, and I was a star on the basketball court. I looked up in the blenchers and saw Shanice sitting there, looking like her world had just come crashing down on her. Anybody who knew Shanice knew she was always wearing the most beautiful smile... that girl lit up my entire world. "Hey babe, what's wrong?" I asked during one of our water breaks. "Nothing we can talk about right now, babe. I'll talk to you after practice. You're doing really well," she said, bragging on my skills. Her voice was sad but she always supported me. "I know! I am, huh? These boys can't see me," I laughed, running back to the sidelines to listen to the coach's talk. He gave a speech about the next game and told us to go home. I'd just gotten my first car a red 2006 Audi A4 maybe a month prior so I felt like the man handing Shanice the keys and telling her to go crank it up and wait for me to get out of the locker room. "Can you not take your boys home tonight?" she asked as I handed her the keys. "Ok, but I have to give Max a ride. He's up in the cafeteria with the geek squad studying," I explained, "and my mom already promised Miss Taylor I'd bring him home." "That's fine. We can talk after you drop him off," she told me. "I'll run up there and get him." Shanice was great to me, and good to my best friend, so there was no way I was going to make her ride with a car full of sweaty guys when she seemed to have so much on her mind. We dropped Max off and, even though I hated driving to Shanice's projects, I did every day just for her. Her grandmother had gotten donations from their church and a few outside sources so she'd be able to pay a full year's tuition for Shanice to go to Forrest Hill. I admired her for that. Shanice's mom was strung out on drugs, and nobody knew who her and her younger sisters' father even was. She'd talked a lot about how she wished someone would tell the man that he had two little girls and maybe he'd come back. Her grandmother had been raising her since birth. Her mom would come to visit them a lot before the drugs took over, which is how she was able to have two of the man's kids without him having an idea about either one. I thought Shanice was about to talk to me about missing her mother, because we had that talk a lot, but I wasn't ready for the bombshell she dropped on me. "What's wrong babe?" I asked, looking into her beautiful eyes. They were her best feature, but then again, she had a lot of best features. "You've been sad all night." "Dan, I'm pregnant," she blurted, looking at me all teary eyed. As much as I wanted to scream it's not mine, I knew that it was. Shanice and I only had sex once. It was the first time for us both, so I said the only thing I knew to be true. "But we used a condom!" "I know," she agreed, with tears brimming in her eyes. "But you were having a really hard time with it... maybe you didn't put it on right." She spoke softly so I'd know she wasn't accusing me' she was just stating facts. "Shanice, I love you and I never want to lose you, but we're only 16. We can't be parents," I responded, looking at her with pleading eyes. "So you want me to give the baby up for adoption?" I could tell that, while she didn't know what she wanted to do yet, she was upset with me for not having the right answers. "No, I could never have a child out there in the world somewhere that I know I didn't want," I admitted. My honesty stung and her tears became more fluid. "Dan, I can't kill this child!" she said, raising her voice, "I'm a Christian, and my grandmother would kill me if I even spoke that nonsense to her." I couldn't believe she had gotten louder with me. "Do you love me?" I needed to handle this situation immediately, before it got out of hand. I knew it was the best thing for not just me, but for the both of us. "You know I do," she answered. "I'll get the money," I promised her. "Your grandmother will never have to know. You're not just doing this for me, Shannie. You're doing this for our futures too." I tried to convince her. She looked at me with those glossy grays and I could tell she was making the hardest decision of her life, a decision I knew she'd never really come back from ...not entirely. "Ok," she said, climbing out of my car without saying another word. I knew she was hurt and, even though the abortion was my idea, she'd never know how hurt I was to know that this would be our only option.

Chapter 32

SHANICE

The past week at Maxwell's had been fun! He'd gone out one day and bought an Xbox One because I told him I wasn't a PlayStation type of girl. We'd played games and kicked it all day. I'd never hung out with Max one on one before, so I had no idea he was so fun to be around. I actually thought he only had fun when he was around Dan. "I'm going to cook breakfast. What do you want?" I asked. I'd heard his stomach growling, which was my cue that it was time to feed my gracious host. "Anything you cook, girl. You had me go buy all that food, so all I'm going to say is it better be a big ass meal," he laughed. Max was a really good friend and supporter. I asked him not to mention Dan's name around me and he didn't, and the one time Dan called, he took the call in another room so I wouldn't have to listen. He'd also given me his credit card so I could get enough clothes and shoes for at least three weeks, and set me up in one of his guest rooms. Had he been interested in my sister, I know her and the kids would have had a good guy around, but I was guessing he was with that girl, Sharon. Max sat on one of the barstools, singing along to the Anthony Hamilton album he had playing over the built in beats sound system he'd gotten installed in the walls of the kitchen, and his voice was amazing. Dan and I told him plenty of times that he should have chosen music over the military, but the military is what helped him pay for school, so we couldn't really argue with that. "Max, you better stop singing… you know I'm vulnerable right now," I joked. The hurt was getting slightly better if I could joke about it, I thought. "I wouldn't take advantage of that," he laughed, smiling at me. It was the first time I had noticed Maxwell looking at me like he could ravage me at any moment. "Well, what if I wanted you to?" I asked. Looking at his face, I could tell he was definitely surprised by my comment. "Wanted me to what?" he asked, acting as if he had no idea what I meant. "Wanted you to take advantage of my vulnerability," I began carefully. "Knowing that I was with your best friend, you wouldn't say no?" I was curious to see if Tameka had been right all along. He stood from his seat and walked a little closer to me. "Shanice, if you said you wanted me to, I'd go through my playlist," he said as he began to scroll through his iPod. "I'd play this song." I heard J. Holiday and Nina Sky begin singing the "Bed" remix. He stepped in so close that our breath became one and when he kissed me, I almost forgot my own name. He stopped the kiss and looked at me with a wanting that I'd never seen, not even on Dan's face. "Do you really want me to take advantage of you?" he asked, his hands touching my bare skin. I was keenly aware of his body just inches from my own, and his scent teased my senses. This was a moment I'd never shared with Max before. I wanted to say yes, but for some reason my lips whispered the word, "No." "I don't believe that," he whispered as he kissed me again and slid his hand gently up my thigh, feeling my wetness all over his fingers. This definitely wasn't the Max I'd known back in school, "but no means no." He backed away and, before I knew what I had done, I was pulling him back into me. He reached behind me, cutting off the two burners I'd turned on to make breakfast, and lifted me up on the counter. He kissed me so passionately, my body couldn't stand it. I wanted him so badly! I lay back on the cold hard counter, not even thinking about how my back would feel later and before I knew it, I felt his tongue flicker on my clit and I almost lost my mind. Dan had begged to do the things I was allowing Max to do, and as much as I wanted to stop him, it felt too good. I threw my head back, placed my hands on the back of his head and enjoyed every moment of it. "You want me?" He lifted his head to ask, but I couldn't speak. All I could do was moan from the effects his tongue was having on me. "Say you want me," he commanded, brushing his tongue against my clit again. "Say you want me, Shannie." He did it again but this time I said what he wanted to hear, and what my body needed me to say. "I want you Max, I want you now!" He pulled his wallet out of the pocket of his sweats and retrieved a condom. I stole this moment to look down at his erection. I had no idea how I'd be able to take it. He was huge and I'd only been with Dan in those eleven years. I prayed Max wouldn't get frustrated with me and stop if I couldn't take all of him. He noticed me staring and started to smile. "Yeah... I'm blessed," he laughed and proceeded to enter me, taking it slowly and still I backed up like virgin school girl. "I have an idea," he whispered softly, picking me up off the counter and carrying me into his bedroom, the biggest bedroom in the house and the only one that was downstairs. He laid me across the bed and that made things a whole lot easier as he entered me. He worked himself in and out of my warmth, hitting spots I had no idea existed. I bit into his shoulder trying not to scream out but it didn't work. "Max! Max!" I yelled his name like I was calling on God. He flipped me around before I knew it and entered me from behind. Lord, what am I doing? I asked myself this question, knowing that the things Maxwell was doing to me now, I'd never allowed Dan to do. He rode me from behind and when he noticed I wasn't used to it, he put me in the superman position, with his body on top of mine. He went as deep as he could and I felt all of him as his manhood seemed to push up and through my stomach. Maxwell was putting in work and I was pleasantly surprised! Our bodies dripping with sweat, he finally exploded in the condom. He went into the bathroom to flush it and I turned over on my side, closing my eyes. "Shannie?" I heard him say my name but pretended to be asleep because I really was too exhausted to talk and I didn't want to hear anything bad. I kind of wondered if he regretted betraying Dan. "Shannie," he whispered again and again. I didn't say a word. "I love you," I heard him say as he kissed me on my cheek and wrapped his arms around me. We fell asleep together.

Chapter 33

MAXWELL

I woke up from my nap with Shanice and headed for the kitchen. I was so hungry, considering we'd skipped breakfast and ended up in bed. I sat at the table with a sandwich and a cup of apple juice thinking about what had transpired between us and praying silently that she didn't wake up with regrets. Just as she entered the kitchen, I was answering a call from Dan. "What's going on, bruh?" I asked, trying not to sound guilty of anything. "Nothing, man... have you heard from Shannie?" he asked, trying to level the tone of his voice so he wouldn't sound so desperate, "I've been trying to call her but she cut her phone off and of course she hasn't contacted me." "Why would she?" I laughed, instantly regretting my flippant response. He'd done the girl terribly wrong and his morals were lacking, but he had been my friend for a long time, although that would likely change soon enough. "This is no laughing matter, Max! I made a big mistake man," he said, sounding angry. "I have to get her back... please tell me you've heard from her." I felt bad for him because, friends or not, I was not going to let Dan stand in the way of my being with Shanice any longer than he already had. "Nah, man," I lied, wishing I hadn't answered the phone at all, "but if I do hear from her I'll let you know." Secretly, I hoped he'd said all that he needed to, so I could get off of the phone. "I appreciate it. So how are you and that girl Sharon?" he asked, changing the subject. I'd been around Dan long enough to know why he was asking and I really just wanted to hang up. Shanice was staring at me with those beautiful greys and the look on her face said we needed to talk, but we couldn't as long as Dan was holding me on the phone. "She wasn't right for me, man," I answered him, apologizing to Shanice with my eyes for being on the phone with Dan when she obviously had something to say, "but I have another girl in mind. I just gotta see what's up." "Look at you! I see you man... tell me how it goes down," he laughed. I knew Dan's enthusiasm was only relief. He was worried that Shanice would run to me, needing shoulder to cry on. Ever since that night at the bowling alley, Dan had been different toward me. "Oh, I will. But hey man, I have to go," I said, changing my voice one that was more urgent, "something just came up." "Aight, bruh," Dan said, sounding relieved as well, "I'll talk to you later." The pleasantries between us had been forced, making the conversation very uncomfortable. I wondered if he had noticed it too, but that was forgotten the moment I lay the phone on its charging pad. My eyes were fixated on Shanice and hers were on me. She was so beautiful, wearing one of my button down shirts, panties, and a pair of footies. She looked better in my clothes than she ever did in Dan's. "I understand if you want me to leave," she said. Her gaze never left mine and I wondered if she were looking at me in a way she never had before. "Leave? What? Why would I want that?" I was confused. All I wanted to do was pull her sexy ass back into my arms and sleep the rest of the day away. "Because, well," she began, her eyes full of sadness again, "Dan..." "Dan isn't here, is he?" I responded sharply, cutting her off. "But... you are best friends." She looked down at the floor, noticeably ashamed, as if following our hearts was the wrong thing to do. "And?" I asked emphatically. How could she not know how important she was to me by now? "Max, I heard you say that you loved me this morning, and I know you were probably speaking out of emotions because of the moment," she reasoned. "You can be honest with me if it was just sex!" Now, she really had me confused and almost upset. How could she think this was just sex? She was the woman of my dreams, the only woman in the world who'd make me willingly betray the trust of my best friend. She has to be kidding! "Shannie, I do love you! I've loved you since the second grade! I purchased this house for you, for us... for the family I hope to someday have with you. How could you ever say that you're just sex to me?" I pulled her into my embrace and looked so deep into her eyes, I felt that our souls were speaking instead. "I just want to give you the love that you've always deserved," I added, kissing her gently until I noticed the tears that were starting to form in her eyes. "What's wrong?" "Nothing, I just... I don't want to be the end of your friendship with Dan." She was still worried about him, and he was the furthest thing from my mind. "You let me handle my friendship with Dan, and understand that you're my muse, my inspiration, you're my reason for living and being successful," I said, pulling her into me. I was glad when she didn't resist, giving me the courage to continue. "Dan is just some dude compared to you. Be my woman, Shanice." I finally said to her what I'd been longing to say for so long. I was finally able to let her know that she was the reason I aimed to be the man that I was. "Okay," Shanice agreed. She spoke softly and the kiss shared between us gave me all the confirmation I needed. Shanice Fuller was finally mine!

Chapter 34

DANDRIDGE

'd been calling around, trying to find Shanice for weeks and nobody seemed to know where she was. I was told by Angel, my maid, that she never returned to the penthouse, not even to get her belongings so I was worried, and I prayed that wherever she was, she was safe. For all I knew, she could still be in Spain. "Ever since that girl left, you have been acting distant. What's wrong now... do you not love me like you said?" Cecelia asked, once again needing confirmation that I really loved her. It was getting old. "Yes Cecelia," I sighed, repeating myself, "I love you. I've just had a lot on my mind with my mom pressuring me to come back home, you, Danny, the new baby. That's the problem with you women, y'all feel like pregnancy and kids don't effect men just because we aren't carrying." I was trying to make her feel bad. "Do you think it would be better?" she asked. "Do I think what would be better?" I responded, clearly annoyed by her strange question. "Moving to America?" she sighed, rolling her eyes. We were on each other's nerves from being around each other constantly. "It would be okay. My family would finally get a little more bonding time with you and the kids," I told her, but in truth, I knew if we went back, I could track down Shanice and win her back. "Okay, well let's plan it. We move to America... but what about your basketball," she asked? "I think it's time to hang up the Nikes. I'm going to apply for Law School, and follow in my father's footsteps," I explained. Shanice had always said I should attend law school as a back-up plan. I'd need it if I were to get injured or decide I wanted to try something different. I had a knack for making people believe my lies, so I'd probably make an awesome defense attorney. I just needed to figure out how I was going to defend myself against Shanice when we finally talked. I knew she'd ask questions about why I'd done this, and I truly had no answers outside of the sex being better, and that was a lame excuse for throwing away eleven years of love and true friendship. "Hello?" I had been surprised, when I reached for the phone, to see that it was a call from my mother. She'd finally decided to return my calls, pulling me away from my thoughts of Shanice and the conversation I was having with my wife. "How's my baby boy?" she crooned into the phone with her sweetest voice, trying to act like things were cool. "I'm good ma," I said, playing along, "talking to Cecelia about moving home." I knew the response I'd get from her. "It sure did take you long enough!" she exclaimed happily. "He's coming home!" she yelled again to whoever was in the room with her. It was likely one or more of my sisters. "I do what's best for my family, ma, not what's best for you... even though here lately, my life has definitely been going your way," I responded, more than a little annoyed by her happiness, only because she always got her way. "Oh son, stop your whining. I did what was best for your family. Got rid of that gold diggin' hussy so you could properly take care of your family." I wanted to curse my mother so bad but I couldn't bring myself to do it. "Okay," I sighed, deciding to let it go before ma became upset and I wouldn't be able to ask her about Shanice. Long as she wasn't mad at me, ma would be thrilled to give me an update on how great she was doing without me in her life. "Did you want anything in particular and do you even know if Shannie is alright?" "I just wanted to say I love you son, and I'm sure she's okay," ma said, sighing as if Shannie was all we'd talked about, "she's probably working down at Sugar Bears." My mom laughed like she'd just made a Kevin Hart type joke. "Shanice would never strip, mom," I responded, already sorry I'd asked, "just forget it." "Ok, ok. I ran into her sister down at Burger King," she said, seizing the opportunity. "She says Shanice is doing well, and already has another man. She's happy son so leave it alone." I could hear the joy in my mother's voice but her words tore through my heart like daggers. How could Shanice move on so fast? It had only been about four weeks. Maybe she'd had someone else all along. As quickly as those thoughts crept into my mind, I knew there was no way she would have done that to me.

Chapter 35

SHANICE

I clapped so hard my hands started hurting as Maxwell received his Master's Degree. It felt good to be there, supporting a man who loved and supported me more than I would have ever guessed. It had been a month since he'd told me he loved me and even with our differences, he showed me how much every day. I felt that I didn't deserve him. His mother wasn't too happy about the way he'd let Sharon fall by the wayside, but the best thing about Miss Taylor was that she supported her son and his decisions. I had no idea how her and Dan's mom were even friends. She'd agreed not to talk about us to Mrs. Harris because Maxwell wanted to be the one to decide when Dan should find out about us. I respected his mother even more for being able to keep other people's business to herself, unlike Mrs. Harris. "I'm so happy you were able to be here," Max said, as he hugged and kissed me. He made me feel so amazing, as if I were the only woman in the world. "Where else would I have been?" I beamed. He looked at me and smiled a gorgeous smile before hugging his mother. She was so kind and supportive; I couldn't wait until that day came, when she'd accept and love me too. "Next stop, the PHD program," his mother said as she squeezed him. He quickly agreed without missing a beat. Maxwell was amazingly smart and very handsome. I never would have thought that he'd turn out to be so fine back in school, but I guess everyone grows up. I couldn't help but feel disappointment that I hadn't recognized how exceptional he truly was, before wasting eleven years on someone like Dan. "Next stop for you, my love, is here," he said sweetly, handing me a business card for Apollo's, one of the top rated restaurants in the Fayetteville area. They had chefs standing in line, trying to get jobs there. "To do what... eat?" I laughed. Max knew I'd already planned a special meal to celebrate his accomplishments. "No," he began, "to work. There is no reason for you to have a culinary degree that you only use in my kitchen. Don't get me wrong. I love you in my kitchen but you're better than that. The first sergeant at my company knew a few people. He talked to them and you start Monday." He hit the nae nae like he'd just pulled off a magic trick. "Please stop dancing," I laughed. "And thanks baby, you're amazing!" I kissed him on the cheek because his mother was standing there. "Anything for you, Mrs. Taylor," he winked. "I love it when you call me that," I said smiling. He made me feel like a school girl whenever I was around him. "One day it'll be real," Max promised, "you just wait!" He kissed me and his mother turned away, looking around like she definitely didn't want to see the affection shared between us, but it was a lovely day and it seemed that we had two things to celebrate. "I can't believe you stole my man," Tameka laughed. I shook my head, wondering if Max should have invited her back to the house for drinks. Always the life of the party, she was sure to embarrass one or both of us, just as soon as the alcohol started kicking in. "I didn't steal anyone," I laughed, shaking my head. "Apparently, he's loved me since we were seven, so ha!" Even though she was a little crass, I enjoyed sharing this day with her, joking and celebrating. "Girl, I told you that man wanted you but you were so stuck up Dan's stank ass, you couldn't even see it," Tameka responded accusingly before taking a sip of her long island iced tea. "And this house, girl? It's so much better than that little fake ass penthouse Dan had you staying in!" "Well, you know it's not about that for me, Meka!" I reminded her in a low voice, shaking my head. Even in my disdain, I couldn't help but smile at my sister's colorful choice of words. "It should be." she said sternly, lifting an eyebrow at me as she sipped her tea, before turning her attention to the room, as if she'd never seen a house of this size before. One thing is for sure, it was always entertaining when Meka's around. I hoped that Max would find her endearing as well. "So when do y'all plan on having kids? Y'all are getting old." My sister was starting to get on my nerves. She felt that everybody needed to be popping out babies, just because she had three. "Later." "How much later?" she pressed. "Late enough! Damn, Meka!" I said emphatically, standing up to refill the ice in my glass. "Just chill! We've been together one month... that's not enough time to start popping out kids!" I looked back to find that she'd already found something else to focus on, other than my womb, and I was relieved. Her head was down, and she was engrossed in Max's Kindle. It was likely she hadn't heard a word I'd said. It was hard to stay upset with Tameka. She means well. I loved hanging out with my little sister whenever we were getting along, which was anytime my mother decided to stay away. We grew up looking out for each other, but Tameka had a very soft spot for mother. Personally, I was done with her until she decided to get herself clean. "Where is Mr. Master's degree anyway?" Tameka asked, looking up from the Kindle and pushing it away. I could see the screen, noticing that she wasn't reading, after all. She was just being nosey, trying to see which titles he'd purchased and which subscriptions he carried. "He went out with his mom's boyfriend to have a few drinks and some male bonding time, I guess," I shrugged. I knew Max didn't have any problems with Rowland, but I also knew that they weren't the best of friends either. He had been spending a little more time with his mom's boyfriend because he was spending less time conversing with Dandridge. I hated that he had to distance himself from his friend. I was ready for him to finally tell Dan the truth. I never really understood why guys would hold on to information until that they were backed into a corner. "Well," she smiled sweetly, "wasn't that nice of him to give you some time to hang with your sister? Girl, you should have been with him this whole time, you was playing." "Well... I guess I'm not playing anymore because I'm happier than I've ever been, and it's all thanks to Maxwell." I felt like I was in a dream world as I expressed my happiness to my sister, and that's when the doorbell rang.

Chapter 36

MAXWELL

"**S**he's the one, man." I smiled like a kid in the candy store as I talked to Rowland. It felt good to have a male figure around, even if it did take 25 years. "I know what you mean," the old man laughed, "your mother is too!" His features were nice for his age, and I could tell he'd lived a clean life. He'd taken pretty good care of himself and, with the exception of his bald head, looked quite a bit younger than he actually was. "You're going to propose to my mom?" I asked. I was shocked. They had only been dating a couple of months, and he already wanted to marry her. I guess I shouldn't be surprised. Ma was a pretty amazing woman. "Yeah, I am," he said admittedly, "Is that okay?" Concern clouded his eyes causing the twinkle to disappear and instantly, I felt bad for reacting differently than I should have, and I quickly recovered. "That's great, congrats!" I said, laughing as I patted him on the shoulder to chase away his concern. "I can tell you make her happy." It wasn't a lie. I was truly happy for my mother. She'd spent so much time raising me that I honestly didn't think she'd ever settle down with anyone. I could tell that Rowland was an interesting man, world traveled, with lots of interesting stories. My ma was always laughing or smiling whenever he was around. He'd slowly been promoted from the guy I'd challenged to a man that had earned my respect. "I want to propose to Shannie but I have no idea how I want to do it," I told him. "I want to make it so special for her. She deserves it." "I'm sure you'll think of something. I think you could drop to one knee in the living room and she'd say yes," Rowland teased. "I can see the love between you two." "I'm not doing no living room proposal man, and you better not give my mom's no living room proposal." We both laughed. "Your mother will definitely get the proposal she deserves," he assured me. I had no doubt that he was telling me the truth. In that moment, I was happier than ever to know she found someone to share her life with. I walked out of the bar with a smile on my face. Thinking about going home to Shanice made me feel like the luckiest man in the world. I silently thanked God for her and, as if she knew she was on my mind, the phone began to ring. "What's up, beautiful," I answered. I could hardly wait to hear her voice on the other end. "I don't know, Maxwell. You tell me," she replied. I could hear attitude all in her voice and had no idea why. "What's going on, Shannie?" My heart felt as if someone had just ripped it from my chest. "Nothing, Max. I just wanted to let you know that, when you get home, I will not be here! You're no different than Dan's lying ass!" Her words felt like daggers being thrown. "Wait a minute, Shanice! Don't compare me to Dan... I am nothing like him. Will you calm down and tell me what's going on?" She was silent for a moment, as if she had to think about telling me or not telling me. "Shannie!" I looked at the phone just as the screen said 'call ended'. I had no idea what I'd done to her, but I was sure as hell going to figure it out.

Chapter 37

SHANICE

I quickly packed my things with the help of my sister. I couldn't believe I'd been so naïve to believe that Maxwell could be the exception to every rule. I should have judged him based off of the fact that he was Dan's best friend, which should have spoken volumes. "Maybe it's not true," Tameka reasoned with me, trying to defend Max. She was trying to choose her words carefully, knowing I was upset. I was determined not to listen to anyone on team Maxwell though. "Whatever, Meka," I mumbled, furiously tossing my belongings into the suitcase. "I've been a fool. I should have known this situation was too good to be true!" Tears started to form in my eyes, even though I was determined not to cry. I'd had a wonderful month with Max and I swore he was different, but I guess I had been wrong again.

Earlier that night...

I opened the door to find a teary eyed Sharon standing before me. I hadn't seen or heard anything about her since the night I dropped in on her and Maxwell. "Hey," I said in no particular tone. "Hey, is Max around?" she asked, trying to look around me. "No," I answered politely, "is there something you need?" I had no idea why she'd be here, but I had a bad feeling about it. "I can just wait on him," she said decidedly, pushing past me like she owned the place. "Um, no. You can tell me what you need with him," I challenged her, "and I'll let him know." "I've been trying to call him and he's not answering, but what I need isn't any of your business," Sharon said, catching an attitude, and that's when Tameka jumped in. "Her man, her business," she blurted, getting in Sharon's face, "so if you aren't talking, you can just wait for Max to call you." I shot my sister a look to let her know I was handling the situation. "Okay, forget it. I came over here to tell him I'm pregnant and he needs to stop ignoring me... because of you!" I couldn't believe she'd snapped at me! "Because of me?" "Yes, because of you!" Sharon spat with tears in her eyes. "If you weren't around, he'd still be with me and he'd be trying to prepare for our child, instead of turning into the same man his father was to him." She rolled her eyes and sat down on the couch, crossing her arms. "So if you don't mind, I'll wait!" I couldn't believe this was happening, and I also couldn't believe that Max would just ignore someone he was so actively involved with, after he'd told me he'd never slept with her. "You know what? You can wait here on the couch, because I'm gone!" I grabbed my sister by the arm and went into Max's room to start packing, but first I needed to call Mr. Taylor and let him know we were done. He and Dan were one of a kind. I couldn't believe it... I thought I had finally found one of the rare good ones.

Chapter 38

DANDRIDGE

"I'll be there in the next couple months," I told my oldest sister Carla. Of the two, I was closer to her and confided more often in her. "I can't believe you've been depressing yourself listening to Missing You," she answered, laughed at me even though it was no laughing matter. I'd been drowning my sorrows in alcohol and love songs, but here lately the only song I wanted to hear was Missing You by Case. That song expressed everything I felt. "Man, stop laughing at me. I let the wrong one go," I spoke truthfully. "Baby bro, you let her go the moment you found out Cecelia was pregnant. After all the two of you have been through, do you think she'd have actually stayed once she found out?" "I know she wouldn't have," I admitted, "but I still have to try." "If you feel it's right," she said

140

slowly, as if thinking of the consequences. I could hear the caution in her voice but I wasn't paying it any attention. Shanice was supposed to be mine. I just wished I would have seen it a long time ago, before I put my heart at risk of losing her for good. "It's right, Carla." "Okay, but I have to go," she replied, sounding as if she'd given up on reasoning with me. "I'm supposed to be meeting your mother for dinner." It sounded as if our mother had been annoying her too. I laughed, glad that it was her and not me. "Alright, love you, sis." "Love you too." I decided to leave home. I'd spent most of the day with Danny while Cecelia and her high maintenance ass friends went shopping. All it seemed to take was my credit cards to make her happy but that was about to stop! I wasn't going to continue to spend money on someone I didn't want to be with. I happened to be on good knowledge that Shanice hadn't closed her bank account, so I got on the phone and made a rather large transfer. When she found out, she'd know I was still thinking about her. It was the only thing I knew to do since I had no clue about her whereabouts and if she'd spoken to Maxwell. He was protecting her. I hated that I had such a loyal best friend because I knew he'd never betray the trust of neither me nor Shanice.

Chapter 39

MAXWELL

"What the hell are you doing here?" I asked, surprised to see Sharon sitting on my couch but it mildly explained why Shanice was not there. "Just visiting," she smiled. The look on her face and the tone in which she spoke told me that was the furthest thing from the truth. I rolled my eyes. "Sharon, please. What did you do?" "I didn't do anything, I promise. I met your little girlfriend for the second time, but I guess she wasn't okay with me dropping by. You know, kind of like she did to me," she challenged me. I could tell by her devilish grin that something had happened; I just didn't know what. I pulled my phone out of my pocket and tried Shanice for the millionth time, but she continued to send me to voicemail. "What do you want, Sharon?" "You look defeated. Hurt even," she smirked. "I'm about ready to hurt you," I warned her. "Why are you here?" "I told you already," she responded, using her most innocent voice, "just visiting." "Okay," I replied to her, raising my voice, "well, cut your visit short and get the hell out!" I was angry and frustrated. I had a crazy bitch in my living room and couldn't get in touch with the woman I loved because of it. Sharon walked past me slowly and once the door was shut behind her, I called my mother. "It's about time you called me, boy!" she answered. She'd been calling me since right before I talked to Shanice, but I'd been ignoring the call because I was trying to reach my woman. "What's going on, ma?" My tone was exhausted and I could tell by her voice that she wanted to chat. "That girl Sharon called me, telling me I was going to be a grandmother," she announced, sounding very excited. "Wait," I responded, knowing I hadn't heard her correctly. "What?" "She said she's six weeks pregnant," ma continued, still talking about Sharon. "Ma, if that girl is pregnant, it's not by me." I shook my head. I couldn't believe Sharon was going around telling people she was having my child. I could count on one hand how many times I'd kissed her. There was no way she was pregnant. "Well, what are you going to do, son?" It obviously wasn't sinking in that she'd been lied to. I'd known Sharon was a little needy and insecure, but I'd never felt she was unstable or capable of this! "I'm not going to do a damn thing but get Shannie back! She came here with those lies and now Shannie is gone. That girl is pressed to be with me," I explained to ma, hoping she'd understand the seriousness of my situation. "Now, Shannie thinks I'm no better than Dan." I wanted to break down in tears, but at the same time I was pissed at Shannie for believing that bullshit so easily, without even asking me anything. I told her I hadn't had sex with that girl. Dan messed her up, and now I was paying the price. I had to figure something out and soon. I didn't want to spend my nights without her by my side.

Chapter 40

SHANICE

"You should answer his calls," Tameka sighed, watching me ignore yet another phone call from Max. "For what?" I demanded. "So he can tell me how sorry he is for not telling me he was about to be a father?" It had been a week and I was still angry. This man had taken my thoughts away from Dan, who was now trying to buy me back and then turned around and hurt me just as much, if not more because I thought he was different. "I'll pass. "He can enjoy his baby mama." My sister picked up my phone and looked at the missed calls. "You've ignored this man 22 times today? It's only 8:00a.m. What man would keep calling you if he wasn't either truly sorry or telling you the truth?" "I know you are team Maxwell but like I said... I'll pass so just drop it," I told her, tired of Max being our only topic of discussion. I had planned on going to work because I'd called out all week, not really caring if I got fired or not. I also planned to start apartment hunting today since I'd just lost two homes back to back, following after some man. "Okay," she said, giving up, "I'll let it go but I don't feel like you're handling this right." She walked to her kid's rooms to make sure they were ready for school because, as always, she was running late. She might have been on time this morning had she not been minding my business. I opened my phone and stared at the picture of Max and myself, lying in bed. I was trying to kiss him while he made a silly looking face. I smiled for a moment, thinking about the time I'd spent with him. I had no idea that I could fall so madly in love in such a short period of time, but Max seemed to be so different from Dan. Dan was the type of guy who felt things had to be done his way or no way at all. He'd always threaten to leave me if I wasn't okay with his plans for us. Now that I look back, I should have just let him go if his plan was to lie and cheat anyway. Max, on the other hand, always included me in decisions. He wanted to know what I saw for us and our future family. He encouraged me to begin working on my career again, and showed me love in ways Dan would have never dreamed. Dan would just throw money at me, thinking that was enough. Max created moments and I enjoyed them. We spent so much time talking, playing games, and I'd listen to him write music and sing. I'd told him that his talent was being wasted but he expressed to me that, by serving in the Army, he was doing something greater and something his kids could be proud of. He'd said he wanted to be their hero and mine. A tear fell from my eye as I thought of the future we weren't going to have. My phone started vibrating again and Max's picture popped up. I wanted so badly to answer, to hear his voice, but I really didn't want to hear the apologies so again I hit ignore.

Chapter 41

MAXWELL

"**D**amnit, Shanice! Answer your phone," I cursed out loud! I'd never known anyone so stubborn. I'd left her so many messages, her inbox was now full and I was running out of ideas. I sent flowers and edible arrangements to her job, only to find out that she'd spent the week away from work. I knew she was at her sister's house so I figured that would have to be my next move, my desperation move. I hated popping up on people because I didn't want to seem like a creepy stalker ex-boyfriend, but Shanice meant way too much to me for me to lose her over a lie. Sharon was outside her mind, creating this turmoil in my life and for nothing! She'd spent the week popping up at my house unannounced, trying to convince me that she was carrying my child like I was an idiot. I'd certainly been off in my judgment to date her, I thought, shaking my head. "Stop denying our baby!" she cried, putting on quite the show. "We did not have sex, Sharon," I reasoned with her, "how are you pregnant?" "So you're just going to keep lying," she said, challenging my last nerve, "still saying we didn't have sex?" I wanted to wrap my hands around her neck for driving Shanice away with those lies. "Please get away from my house before I call the cops," I'd threaten. She'd leave and we did this over and over every day. I finally decided to contact Dan's father to help me get a restraining order. I felt like Sharon wasn't pregnant at all. If she could convince herself that we had sex, I was sure she could convince herself of a nonexistent child. "What are you doing here?" I'd arrived at Tameka's just in time to catch Shanice, just as she was walking out of the house. "I needed to see you," I pleaded with her. "To tell you what's been going on..." "Look, I'm really not in the mood to be lied to or played. I spent eleven years being down for the bullshit," Shanice replied coldly. Her tone was raw but the way she looked at me, I knew she hadn't stopped loving me yet. "Shannie, that woman is lying. I know Dan hurt you and lied to you but I'm not him. I love you way too much to treat you the way that he did." She rolled her eyes. "What reason does she have to lie on you, Max?" "She's out of her mind, that's what reason. She convinced herself that we had sex and created a child. I barely kissed her, let alone had sex with her." Shanice looked at me like I was the crazy one. "Look," she began, noticeably irritated, "when you're ready to own up to your shit, you clearly know where to find me." She tried to brush past me but I caught her arm, and pulled her into me. The heat between us was almost unrealistic. "Shannie, please don't do this to us. If you walk away from me, you will regret it! You will regret not believing the one man who would literally lay down his life for you. I've put my friendship of eleven years on the line because I love you. Do not walk away from me," I warned her. My tone was firm yet bearing the truth of my love for her. She looked at me and I decided to kiss her. I could tell she was lost in the kiss because, for at least five seconds, time seemed to stop around us, and I knew I'd won. Until she pulled away from me, and my arms felt so empty. "Bye, Maxwell." She stepped around me and for the first time in years, I cried. I felt like my heart had been ripped from my chest and set ablaze. How could she just walk away from me? How could she just let what we had go?

Chapter 42

SHANICE

couldn't believe Max would come to me, making up lies about Sharon. Would he really go that far as to make that woman seem crazy just to be with me? I loved Max, but I couldn't be with another liar, so I decided I'd give Sharon a call so I could hear her side of the story. Sharon and I decided to meet at Christine's Wine and Burger Bistro in Durham because she'd been showing houses there. I hated driving to Durham and I also hated the crime rate there but being from where I was from, I knew how to handle myself if things got out of hand. I walked into the dimly lit restaurant and felt more like I was on a date than a lunch meeting. It was very nice, and so expensive that the prices weren't even listed on the menu. Being with Dan, I was used to these types of places but being who I am, I hated spending large amounts of money on food I could easily cook at home. The waitress led me to a table in the corner by a window where Sharon was sitting. As I sat down in front of her, I was able to look at her for the first time. Every other encounter I'd had with Sharon, I barely noticed her. I knew she was very pretty but looking at her now, the woman was gorgeous, reminding me a lot of my sister, the two of them were almost identical. People knew that Tameka and I had the same dad, but her golden complexion and nearly hazel eyes would never suggest her mixed-race at all, whereas my eyes were always a dead giveaway. "So you called me here... what do you want?" Sharon's rude attitude brought me back to reality. "I just want to know your side of the story and if you're making this whole thing up about Max. Max is a good man..." my sentence was cut short by her rolling her eyes and coughing. "As I was saying, Max is a good man and I just can't believe he'd get you pregnant and then just walk away." "You drove all the way to Durham to say that?" she asked, snapping at me. "Why are you so rude?" I asked, getting frustrated. "Rude? You're calling me rude? You waltz in Maxwell's house one day and never leave, but I'm rude. I've left you alone for a long time now," she added, glaring at me, "why don't you do the same for me?" "All I want to do is find out the truth, woman to woman. Why can't you just give me that much?

It's not too much to ask." "Shanice, sweetie," Sharon responded, obviously hoping to insult me, "you wouldn't know the truth if it slapped you into next week. I'm late for an appointment. Thanks for wasting my time." "I'll take that in a to-go box," she told the waitress as she came to the table with our food. I didn't know what Sharon and Max were hiding but I knew it was time I let it go and move forward. Maybe Sharon wouldn't be so ugly and hateful once she had her man back.

Chapter 43

DANDRIDGE

"You still love her!" Cecelia yelled at me after catching me staring at the one picture of me and Shanice that I'd held on to. "I love you," I responded not wanting to argue. It was all we seemed to do lately. I chose to keep my marriage and we'd had two good weeks after that, and then the continuous arguing started. "I am not going to America if you are only trying to get her back," she announced, folding her arms across her chest. I'd had enough. I'd finally decided to show her a side of me she'd really never seen before. I was tired of feeling like I was Cecelia's bitch. "Okay," I challenged her, "don't go, but come next Friday... me and my daughter will be gone. You can't keep Danny from spending time with her father's family, so you can choose." "You will not take my daughter anywhere!" Cecelia screamed. "Your daughter? So are you saying she's not mine?" I asked, only wanting to further piss her off. There was definitely no doubt that Danny was my daughter. She looked like I'd given birth to her myself. "Asshole," she said, walking away like I knew she would. I decided to call my mother to see if she had any more information than she'd had the first time we'd talked. "Hey son," mom answered, sounding unusually happy. "How are you?" "Miserable... you?" I was quire curious what had my mother sounding so chipper. "Oh Dandridge," she giggled, acting as if I'd told her something extremely funny, "please stop! I'm wonderful. Your father has finally sent me divorce papers after all these years, and has agreed to give me alimony!" I should have known that her happiness had something to do with my father's money. I loved my mother to death but she definitely was not the type of woman I'd ever want to be with myself. She was selfish and it wasn't until recently that I realized she'd raised me to be the same way. "I'm happy for you," I lied. "Well then sound like it! Put some pep in your voice, young man!" "That's not what I called you for ma," I reminded her, changing the topic. "Have you done what I asked you to do?" "I've done that and more," she laughed. I had no idea what that meant but I was sure she'd be quick to tell me. Mom was quite the drama queen when she wanted to be. "So?"

I asked, getting annoyed. "Who is Shanice in a relationship with, mom?" "Nobody!" I could hear my mother cackling with delight, but I wasn't finding anything about this conversation funny and her silly games were making no sense. "You just told me she was in a relationship last week," I said, trying to control my voice, "now you're telling me she's not. Why are you playing these games?" "She was in a relationship last week ...and this week she's not," she explained coyly, taking a deep breath to feign annoyance. "I don't know why you are so in love with that girl. Do you know how broken she is? Do you know how much of a mess her family is? Do me a favor, son. Come back and leave the whores where they are." I couldn't believe my mother! "I've taken care of Shanice. She'll be way too busy with her own messed up life to deal with you," she promised. I could feel my blood boiling, knowing I would be angry with her, whatever it was. "Taken care of her? What have you done, mom?" I asked, fearing it was something really bad. "What are you talking about?" "Nothing!" she said in a singsong voice, her happiness was getting on my nerves now. "I have to go now. I love you, son... can't wait to see you next week!" She hung up the phone before I had the chance to further question her, but I had no idea what she'd meant by taking care of Shanice. I also had no idea why she'd still be concerned with Shanice's life. My mom had to have done something shady and I was going to find out what, as soon as I got back but for now, I figured I'd give Max a call. It was time for me and my best friend to get back on good terms. He'd been so distant toward me since he found out I was married. I couldn't lose my girl and my best friend. I knew Max would be far more forgiving.

Chapter 44

MAXWELL

"Hello?" I looked at the clock and noticed it was 4:00a.m. I had to be up within the next hour to head to PT. Whoever this was, it had better be important. "What's up man?" I heard Dandridge on the other end. "You do know I work right?" Rude I know, but every time my phone rang and it wasn't Shanice, I found myself in a worse mood. "My bad, bruh," he said apologetically, "time difference. Want me to call later?" "No, you good man," I responded, trying to be less hateful, "what's on your mind?" "Nothing," he replied, "just trying to catch up, see if you've heard from Shanice." I should have known that the only reason he'd be calling me was to talk about her. "No, I haven't," I answered dryly, trying to control my emotions. Just knowing that I hadn't heard anything from her since the other day when I'd stopped by her sister's house was killing me inside. "Ok, well how's that new girl you were telling me about?" Dan asked, trying to be friendly. I just didn't have much of anything to say. "Over before it started, my friend," I answered truthfully. "Well, there's someone good out there for you, bruh," he offered. "Don't worry." "I'm not worried at all," I lied. I was worried. I was worried that I would never be able to get Shanice back. I was worried that Dan would one day find out I was the next man Shanice shared her bed with and we'd lose our friendship. I had no idea what I was thinking, putting my friendship on the line for Shanice's unstable ass. My thoughts were starting to get the best of me and every positive thought I had toward Shanice had to turn negative because if it didn't, I'd be in a bad position ...and because I was in a leadership position in my unit, I could not be walking around with all these crazy emotions. "Well, I'll be home next week. I want to introduce you to my family," he promised. "Well... mainly my little girl. She's my twin." I was surprised to hear the pride in my friend's voice. I wanted to let him know that I'd heard. The first few days that Shanice had stayed with me, she talked my ear off about Dan and that little girl. She told me how she wondered if their child would have looked as much like him as she did. "Sounds like a plan," I replied, "but hey, I have to go ...got PT formation." "Yeah man," Dan sighed. "See you next week." We hung up the phone and I started talking to God. I prayed that whatever was for me, He'd give it to me and in His time, and if it was for Shanice to walk away so that Dan and I could keep our friendship, then so be it. My loyalty to Dandridge had never been in question till now. I was going to have to choose which road I wanted to pursue. Those two roads were fairly clear to me now. It was either get my friendship back on track or chase a woman who clearly didn't want to be caught.

Chapter 45

SHANICE

I sat in my grandmother's kitchen while thinking and trying to piece together all of the things that had taken place over last month. It had been the most hectic and trying month of my life. I'd lost two men I loved and I felt that I'd gained nothing. Yes, Max had encouraged me to start my career again but cooking felt dead without him. He made me feel alive while I cooked. He'd always sit in the kitchen, singing to me, flirting with me, touching me, sometimes out right distracting me so we could make love. I sat there, thinking about Max and how he'd touched me in ways that Dan couldn't. How could he be just as bad a guy?

Last Month...

Maxwell walked into the kitchen, wearing nothing but his lounging pants and with good reason; he had the body of a Greek God. "What are you cooking," he asked as he walked over to the stove smelling like he'd just stepped out of the shower. "A little of this and a little of that," I answered playfully. "Well, this and that smells good," he teased, complimenting me. "So do you," I smiled. "You should taste me," he added, looking down at the front of his pants where there was a hole for his penis. "Max," I began, "you know I've never..." "Just because you've never done it doesn't mean you can't start now, or that you won't be good at it. You fuck me like a porn star nowadays." Max was clearly trying to boost my confidence. "That's just because you're patient with me, not because I'm a natural." I appreciated his efforts and loved the way he made me feel wanted. "Okay and I will be patient with you now. You don't have to," he answered, walking around the counter to his normal seat and I was amazed that he didn't have an attitude. I was impressed that a man could be this understanding. Dan always stormed out whenever he didn't get what he wanted sexually. I cut off the burners I had going and told myself I'd finish cooking later. I walked over to Max and kissed him gently. "What's that for?" Max had asked. "Just for understanding," I answered, massaging his penis through his pants until I could tell he was rock hard. The barstool was too high so I asked him to stand up so that I could at least get on my knees to gain access to him. "You know you don't have to do this," he assured me. "I want to. Feed me Max," I said before even realizing how dirty it sounded, but the way his eyes lit up, I knew he liked the dirty comment. I took him into my mouth, not quiet able to fit all of him in, but I took in as much as I could and began to suck. I used my tongue around the head and he grabbed my head with his hands, moaning to let me know I was doing it right. He began to pump himself in and out of my mouth as if he was inside of me, and even though I gagged a few times, I started to get the hang of the motion and how he wanted it done. "I'm about to... about to," I knew he was about to cum and even though my first thought told me to move, I wanted Max to know I was all in. Within moments, his warm sperm trickled down my throat and he laid back into the chair, almost falling over. "Girl, that was amazing," he smiled. "You really enjoyed it?" I'd asked him. "Did I? Now as soon as I'm able to walk, I'm going to take you in our room and make love to you, just to show you how much I enjoyed it." We went into the bedroom and I watched as he massaged his own dick, and he watched me play with myself; it was something he enjoyed so I'd become quite comfortable playing with myself in front of him, just to turn him on. I licked my wet sticky fingers, tasting myself, and that's when he joined me in bed. He kissed me so passionately; I almost had an orgasm just from the kiss. He entered me and began to put in work, as he often did. I whispered for him to pull out when he was almost there because I noticed that, this time, he didn't put on a condom. "I will, I promise," he whispered, as he continued to make love to me like there was no other woman in the world. He felt himself about to explode and, just as he promised, he pulled out and released himself onto my stomach. As gross as I thought it was, I didn't mind. I wanted all of Max; I wanted Max in ways that I had never wanted Dan.

Chapter 46

MAXWELL

As the warm water from the shower beat down on me, I was happy to feel her behind me, gently massaging my back. I'd missed her touch, her scent, but most of all her love. "I love you," I said as I turned to face her. "I love you too Maxwell." I loved when she called me by my full name. She was the only person who did other than my mom. I leaned down to kiss her deeply, passionately. I needed her to know how much I missed her, how much I longed for her. I cupped her ass in my hands and pressed myself against her so she could feel my growing manhood between her legs, and know that I was about to make love to her like I'd never done before. I was going to give it to her so well that she'd never want to leave me again. We stepped out of the shower and she allowed me to dry her off as I got around her ass, I dropped the towel to the floor. Wrapping my arms around her, I allowed my fingers to massage her forbidden place until she moaned from the feeling. I kissed her neck gently and waited for her to beg for me; she did. I lifted her off her feet and carried her to my bed where I began to devour her, saving her juices on my tongue as if I'd need them later. I bit down on her clit softly, being careful not to hurt her, but providing her with the perfect sensation. "Maxwell," she purred my name and I almost exploded from the sound. "Maxwell," she said again but this time it sounding more like a question. "Maxwell," she got a little louder and I knew her time was coming. "Maaaaaaaax," she moaned as she arched her back to ride her orgasmic wave. When she was done, without warning or hesitation I lifted myself and entered her slow and deep. "Ooooh," she moaned as she bit down on her bottom lip and made a face that told me I could feel at home inside of her. Body to body, I worked myself in and out slowly as she moved her hips, matching my rhythm. She was so wet, it was almost like being on a slip and slide, but better. She started to contract her muscles around the head of my penis and I could barely take it; she was so tight and warm. I didn't know a man that wouldn't have exploded as soon as they entered her but because she was mine; there was no way I'd only give her a few minutes of pleasure. I went as deep as I could and she started grinding herself on me, riding from the bottom. At that point, I was a goner as I allowed her to move. She worked her hips and before I knew it, we were both at our climax. It felt like a fantasy... we were coming at the same time! "Having that dream again?" I heard a familiar and unwelcomed voice, forcing my eyes to focus in the darkness. "If I call the police right now, your crazy ass is going to jail!" I threatened, with no idea how Sharon had even gotten in. "You were moaning in your sleep," she smirked. "Were you remembering what we had?" I wanted to slap the black off of her. Truth was, I'd been having the same sex dream about Shanice for over two weeks. She still wasn't talking to me and Sharon was still being crazy. I wanted to have her locked up because she continued to violate the restraining order, but I really needed to know her aim. "Why won't you leave me alone?" "Because I loved you, and you hurt me! You're no better than your no good father!" she said, lashing out in an effort to insult me. "Okay, Sharon," I sighed angrily, knowing it was time to end this intrusion. "I'm calling the police. I'm tired of you overstepping your bounds." "I'll go," she lashed out, her eyes shooting daggers my way, "but trust and believe, you'll see me again because you are going to take care of your baby!" She walked over to the bedroom window and looked outside, as if she were expecting someone. "I don't have any kids!" I said, raising my voice. I was getting tired of being accused of something I hadn't done. She lifted her shirt and I could see the small baby bump, so I knew she was definitely pregnant. My shocked expression obviously pleased her. Still, I just knew the baby wasn't mine. I wondered who had knocked her up that quickly after we'd said our good-byes. Something was definitely off in this situation and I was curious to find out what it was. I had to give my boy Dan a call. He'd already been back home for a couple of weeks and we'd barely had time to catch up. This weekend would be a good time to change that.

Chapter 47

DANDRIDGE

I walked into my mother's house and she was nowhere in sight, so I knew exactly where to find her... outside by the pool. I'd noticed a black 745 BMW outside so I knew she had company. I was just praying I didn't find her in some compromising position out there with some man. My mom was so happy about her divorce and alimony, she was starting to act like a young tender and I still had no idea of what she'd been talking about when she said she'd taken care of Shanice. I just knew I couldn't find my woman. I walked into the backyard and was shocked to see Sharon, the realtor, sitting with my mother. They were laughing and talking like they'd known each other from way back. "Hey son!" mom immediately greeted me. "Let me introduce you to..." "I remember... Sharon," I said, interrupting my mother. "We've already met." "Hi Dan," Sharon responded. "It has been a while, hasn't it? How are you?" She was acting very familiar, as if we'd met more than once. "I'm okay. So, what are you doing here?" I happened to be on very good knowledge that she was trying to pen her kid on my boy Maxwell, so she was one of the last people I was about to get all comfy cozy with. "Your mother hired me as your realtor... she didn't tell you?" I looked in my mom's direction and she smirked, quite pleased with herself for meddling in my business. "Mom?" "Well, she found such a lovely house for Maxwell. I figured she could help you and Cecelia," she replied innocently. Instantly, I got the feeling that something wasn't right. "I can find my own realtor, but thanks," I said to mom, before turning to relieve Sharon from her position as my realtor. "Sorry my mom wasted your time, Sharon, but I think you should leave." "No, no," my mom argued politely, shaking her head. "She should stay. Just give her a chance, son. The two of you have more in common than you think, so I think she'll be a good realtor for you." My mom's grin was more devious than convincing. "No offense... but this bawd is crazy," I responded, hoping mom would get the point this time. "I'm good." "You only know one side of the story, so don't judge me," Sharon quipped, defending herself. "How about we do lunch tomorrow? Hear my side... and you still don't want to work with me, we'll call it quits." She must have thought she was talking to a fool. "Don't need to hear your side," I told her, growing more annoyed with each comment she made. "I don't want to work with you." "I'm sure you'll want to hear my side," Sharon smirked. "My side includes your ex. Shanice, isn't it?" I almost pushed her into the pool just for mentioning Shanice's name, as if she knew her. I didn't know what my mother had told Sharon, or what she'd offered, but I was sure it wasn't good. Still, if she knew something about Shanice I wanted to know what it was. "Okay. Lunch tomorrow... McDonalds. One o'clock. Don't be late because I will leave," I warned. My voice was stern so she'd know I wasn't playing. My mother stood there, looking quite satisfied. "I'll be there." Sharon smiled sweetly and walked away as if she'd just won a battle.

Chapter 48

SHANICE

I couldn't believe I'd just received the head chef job at Christine's! After my conversation with Sharon, and coming to the conclusion that I needed to get away from Fayetteville, I'd decided to talk to Christine, the owner. Come to find out, her head chef was about to leave for a job cooking abroad and she was looking for someone to fill the position. She allowed me to cook a few things for her, which was cool because I didn't want to feel like I'd driven an hour and a half just for a short lunch that didn't go anywhere. Christine gave me a call back to let me know that I could start next week, which excited me beyond belief. It may not have been as far away from Maxwell and Dan as I wanted to be, but it was far enough for the moment. It didn't take me long to find a nice condo in Cary, thanks to the money that Dan had been wiring me while trying to get my attention. I gladly accepted the money but did not contact him. I was a bit hurt that Max had stopped calling, but I couldn't be too mad. I hadn't answered a single one of his calls since I'd left him. I just couldn't take it, and hearing his voice would have broken me to the point of no repair. "So, you're sure you don't want to talk to either one of them before you leave?" my sister asked as we loaded the last box into my car. "I'd love to see Max, but I can't handle it. Dan should have just kept his trifling ass in Spain," I commented with much attitude. Dan's family was very well known so it didn't take any time for me to find out he was back. I also knew that the first thing he'd done when he got back was hit a bar with Maxwell. I knew Max didn't have the balls to tell Dan about us, but I wasn't too concerned, considering it was over before it ever even got started. "Sister to sister, and seriously speaking, I really think you should go talk to Max one more time before you leave," Tameka reasoned. "I really don't think he's the dude that you've made him out to be in your head." I knew my sister was right but I didn't know if I could forgive him for wanting to walk out on his kid, just to be with me. Maxwell was being selfish and the child didn't deserve that. "No, he needs to step up and do for his kid." "So you can't be in his life and let him step up?" she said, challenging my decision. "I'm not playing stepmother to anybody's child," I told her with conviction. I never saw myself helping to raise kids that didn't belong to me, and I wasn't going to see it now just because it was Max. "Sometimes the fairytale comes with a little extra baggage." Tameka's words hit me kind of hard but not hard enough to change my mind. "Well, sometimes people come with baggage you're not willing to help them unpack," I told her as I rifled through my purse for the keys. "I love you little sis. Take care of my nephews and my niece. I'll be home in a few months... I'm just trying to stay away from here as long as possible. And tell grandma I left some money for her in the cookie jar." I hugged my sister and got in my car; it was time for Shanice to have a fresh drama free start.

Chapter 49

DANDRIDGE

I sat in the bowling alley on post, trying to enjoy myself with Max but after the conversation I'd had with Sharon earlier that day, I just could not focus. I wanted to ask Max a lot of questions about what happened between him and Shanice but every time I brought her name up, he'd dismiss me, telling me I needed to worry about my wife and fixing my marriage since that's what I'd chosen. I kept asking myself what Maxwell could be hiding, because he wasn't himself lately, and it seemed that everybody around here had secrets. Not just me, although mine seemed to be the biggest secrets of all.

Earlier that day...

I sat at a corner booth in McDonald's, waiting on Sharon to get her food. Normally I would have paid for it but I didn't like anything about this shady girl, and the fact that she'd been hanging with my mom definitely did not help. She sat down at the table with a snide grin on her face like she was about to give me life changing information. As much as I didn't want to buy into her game, her words hit closer to home for me than they should have. "So what's going on? What's your side of the story? I don't have much time," I asked, jumping straight in. I wanted to get this meeting over with. "I just wanted to tell you that Shanice stayed with Max for a month, after the two of you split." I looked at her blankly, wondering if this was the big secret she'd been so willing to share. "They're friends. And? What does Max looking out for Shanice have to do with you pinning a baby on him that's not really his?" "He's sleeping with her," she said matter-of-factly and I fell out laughing. I knew for a fact that Max would not betray our friendship in such a way, and I also knew that Shanice had never been interested in Max, so that was a good try but not good enough. "So, how much is my mother paying you to try ruining my life?" I asked. "Because I know that's a lie, just like the lie you're telling about being Max's baby mama!" She looked and me and shook her head as if I were the one that was crazy. "Look," Sharon said, leaning in closer so no one would overhear. "I have some connections. Some people who have a lot of money and a lot of pull. This most certainly is Maxwell's baby." She was smirking now, and obviously very proud of herself. "I don't believe that the people you know are able to pull sperm out of the air," I replied, challenging her. I wanted to know why this girl was so hell bent on having Max father her child. "Or," she smiled again, "maybe they can." "Stop playing games, Sharon." When I'd first seen this girl, I'd been surprised at how pretty she was but now, staring across the table, she was probably one of the homeliest I'd ever met. I couldn't stand her know-it-all attitude and constant smirking. "What are you talking about? There's only one way for you to be pregnant and I know my boy. So," I countered, "if he says he didn't sleep with you, he's not lying." "I don't know when and I don't know how," she whispered, but it sounded more like a hissing sound when she spoke, "but my connection assured me that the sperm was indeed Maxwell's." I was in pure shock. "You went to a sperm bank?" "Sure did! So this baby I'm carrying may not be a love child but it's his child," she responded, cackling so hard I thought she'd lose her voice. Sharon was carrying somebody's baby alright, but it sure wasn't Maxwell's, as she so whole heartedly believed.

The Present...

"You bowling or what man?" Max was talking to me and I'd zoned out. "Oh yeah man, my bad... got some stuff on my mind," I said, trying to forget the crazy lies that Sharon had told me. "What's up bruh?" Maxwell asked. "It's nothing worth talking about. But that girl Sharon tried to tell me you and Shanice had a thing going on," I laughed and he joined in. "Nah, man," he assured me, "why would she say that?" "That girl is crazy about you, man." "That's obvious," he laughed as he shook his head, "but no, you have nothing to worry about. Me and Shanice don't even talk. I was just an ear when you hurt her, man. That's it." He assured me and I believed him; he'd never been one to lie to me before. As long as I'd known Max, he'd always kept things straightforward and honest, which was why we bumped heads as often as we did. We were like brothers.

Chapter 50

MAXWELL

I couldn't believe I'd just lied to Dan. In my heart, I really did feel like Shanice had used me to get over her broken heart. Like the saying goes, the best way to get over one man was to get under another. I wished it wasn't true but in this case, I felt it was. She didn't even give me a chance to explain and worst of all, she knew me better than most people but chose to believe some stranger over me! There was no way she loved me like she'd said she did. I knew Dan's actions had crushed her but damn! Did that mean I couldn't get the benefit of the doubt? I guess not. I knew that one day, the truth would come out but I wasn't ready to lose a friend until I had Shanice as my wife, but right now, she just some girl I was chasing, and trying to win back. "Dude, you seem real distracted. What's up?" I asked Dan. The more we chilled, the more he seemed to keep floating off into another world. "Can I ask you something, man?" Finally, I thought. Maybe I'd find out what had him acting so distant. "Yeah, man ...anything," he assured me. "You remember when we were 16 and I asked you if I could use your name to donate sperm? And we went to the sperm clinic?" I shook my head and smiled, waiting for him to get to the point. Remember how I lied and told them I was 18 so I could make some money without having to go through my parents?" Dan asked. I was confused as to why he would even be thinking of this now, when he obviously had plenty of money and his second child on the way, but I was curious. "Yeah... why?" "I wonder if we got any kids out there wishing they had a dad," he said, looking real serious. "We?" What was he trying to lead up to, I wondered. "I mean... your name was on it," he laughed. "Yeah," I laughed, remembering that day, "but your sperm was in the cup, my friend, so you should be wondering if you've done what God asked of Noah and replenished the earth and shit." We both laughed. "I hope not," he said as an afterthought before taking a swig of his beer, but I could tell he had some heavy thoughts going on. "I thought we agreed that would never come up. What made you think of it now?" I really wanted to know where that unplanned trip down memory lane had come from. "No reason, man," he told me. "It was just a random thought." He turned his attention to the server to request another round of drinks. I knew when Dan was lying and he was definitely lying, but I decided not to press the issue. I had bigger things on my mind than why Dan was all of a sudden into his feelings about sperm that was donated when we were kids. We left the bowling alley a little after midnight and I caught a cab to Tameka's house, praying Shanice would talk to me. I had everything in the world to say to her and I figured the liquid courage I'd had with Dan would help me. The cab stopped in front of the house and the little red Honda coupe that Shanice drove was nowhere in sight, but I knocked on the door anyway. "Max, what are you doing here?" Tameka opened the door in her house coat and I could tell she was angry. I didn't even think about the fact that I might disturb her kids. "Sorry Meka," I answered her, feeling bad that I hadn't been very considerate. "I was looking for Shanice." "She moved. I'm sorry, Max." I could tell that she really cared. "Moved?" I responded, raising my voice. "Moved where?" "Shhh!" she said, before you wake the neighborhood! Look. I'm not supposed to be telling you this, but I feel like my sister is being foolish." She stepped inside the house and wrote something down, thrusting the paper into my hand. "Here's her address." It was in Cary, which was close to an hour and a half away. "Thanks," I smiled. Shanice was running away from the situation here instead of facing it, so I figured soon she'd be getting an unexpected visitor. I walked out into the front yard and after that, everything just went black.

Chapter 51

SHANICE

I opened my front door to find Max sitting outside. "What are you doing here? How'd you even get my address?" I had a pretty good feeling as to how, but I wanted him to tell me. "I'm trying to decide if it would be wise to ring your doorbell ...and I got your address from around the way," he snapped, trying to be smart. "What do you want, Maxwell?" "Isn't it obvious?" he asked. "I want you!" "So what?" I asked him, visibly perturbed, but my heart raced at the sight of him on my doorstep. "You're just going to stalk me until you totally creep me out, and every feeling I have for you vanishes for good?" "So you admit that you still have feelings for me?" He stood up to approach me, and before we were even close, I could feel the heat between us rise, just as it always did whenever Max got close to me. "No," I lied. "Come on, Shanice. Stop playing these games," he scolded, getting all the way in my face. "I'm not playing stepmom to your kid, Max," I said in barely a whisper. "I don't have any kids," he responded softly, defending himself. Before I could respond, his lips connected with mine and I had no will to resist him. He gently but firmly pushed me back into the condo, and kicked the door shut making sure not to break our kiss. I'd missed him so much, but I didn't know if I'd be able to handle him and his drama. "You want me, don't you?" he whispered. "No," I lied again. "Say you want me, baby," he begged. "No, I don't want you." I could barely utter the lie in between breaths. He unbuckled the pants I had on and sat me on the edge of the couch. I kept saying no ...but I was not resisting. "Say you want me, Shanice," he coaxed. "No, Max," I started. "I don't. I don't..." He cut me off by burying his tongue inside of me. "I want you, Max," I heard myself say and he began to devour me as if he hadn't eaten in weeks ...or even months. I felt him stick his finger inside of me as he continued to drive me crazy with his tongue. I came all over his mouth and couldn't seem to stop shaking. I wanted Max so bad it was killing me. "Come here," I commanded him softly, lifting his face to look into my eyes. I wanted him to see how bad I wanted him. I needed him inside my love, penetrating me slow, and deep. He came up and kissed me as I used my feet to push down his sweats and boxers; he was rock hard and ready. "I don't have a condom," he whispered. "Max, I want you... all of you." I looked into his eyes and he entered me slowly, just like he always did before he got into his natural motion of making love to me, of pleasing me, of bringing me to orgasm after orgasm. He flipped us over and I began to ride him, looking at every expression on his face. I loved this man and I wanted him to know it. There was no other man for me, there was only Max. I grinded on him until I noticed he couldn't take it. He held on to my hips as tightly as he could. "Baby, get off," he said but I didn't listen. I contracted my muscles around him one last time and he released his seed into me as I collapsed onto his chest. I felt bad because I knew how much I loved Max and how much he loved me, but I had no clue how this could work.

Chapter 52

MAXWELL

I woke up and looked at Shanice, sleeping peacefully beside me. The couch wasn't really big enough to accommodate us both, but it was cool being cuddled up with her again. I'd missed her so much. "What?" she asked as she looked up to find me staring at her. "Nothing... just happy to have my girl back," I smiled. "Max, we aren't back together." "What?" I couldn't believe what I was hearing. There was no doubt that Shanice still loved me ...and clearly, I loved her. "Maybe we just made a mistake," she murmured, looking down so I couldn't connect with those beautiful greys that never seemed to lie. "So... what is this? I come over. We have sex and you want me to just leave like it never happened?" I could feel my temperature rising. "Not like it never happened," Shanice began, trying to choose her words carefully, "because it was amazing, but I do want you to leave. I didn't invite you here in the first place and this is why." I couldn't believe what I was hearing. Shanice was tripping. "Shanice, please stop with these games because I promise you, you will not be happy if I decide to let you go and move on. You know we're made to be together, but I'm not going to keep chasing you if you truly don't want to be caught," I said, trying to warn her. "Well, stop then, Max," she pleaded sadly. "Just leave me alone." The words she spoke didn't match the look in her eyes. "You don't mean that." I demanded, glaring at her. "I love you Max," she replied, "but you have some drama you need to deal with, and I don't feel you can if I'm around." I wanted to throw something. "So, you mean to tell me that you could hold down a trifflin' nigga like Dan for eleven years... this man made you abort a baby, and hell I may have just given you one, and you can't have my back? You can't believe in me the way you believed in a man you knew meant you nothing good?" I was hurt beyond measure. "Well, maybe if I wouldn't have held Dan down, I'd feel differently." Her response was cold. I watched as the tears ran down her face but I couldn't understand why she was crying. "You're crying but your pain is your choice," I told her. "I'm done with this." I walked out with revenge on my mind. Dan would pay for hurting her so badly, and for ultimately destroying the happiness that I'd been praying for, for so long. Forget loyalty, Dan and I were no longer boys.

Chapter 53

DANDRIDGE

"I can't do this anymore," I told Cecelia. "Do what?" She looked confused and I had to remember she wasn't an American. She wouldn't automatically assume that I was talking about us. "I think you're a real special woman, Cecelia, and I will continue to support our children, but I want a divorce." I was as honest as I could be. "You will continue to support our children?" Cecilia asked, her voice shrill. "Dan, I will take you for everything you have!" I was surprised that she had tried her hand at threatening me. "No, actually you won't," I countered. "Remember, the prenuptial agreement? You leave with what you came with, sweetheart." "You cold bastard!" my wife cried, tears pouring from her eyes like a waterfall. I almost felt bad... not because I was leaving her but because I'd moved her to the States only to tell her I was done with her. I'd lived a lie long enough and I knew that I wouldn't have a chance with Shanice if I was still with Cecelia, because she'd most definitely ask. "I'm also going to see about joint custody of the kids. I don't want them spending their entire lives in Spain and not getting a chance to know their father or my family," I added, speaking to her in a matter-of-fact tone. "Fuck you, Dan," she said, walking away, but I knew she wasn't going far. My condo wasn't that big. I pulled up in front of Christine's Wine and Burger Bistro about three hours after telling Cecelia that we were over. It had been a while since I'd seen or talked to Shanice, and it took a lot of work to find out where she was hiding these days, but her mother would tell you anything for a few dollars. I walked into the restaurant and was in awe at how nice it was. Too bad she won't be here long, I thought to myself, knowing that I was going to get her back soon and we'd be right back in the place we were, before all of this drama happened between us. "How many?" the cute little receptionist asked. "Oh no, sweetheart," I smiled, charming her out of habit rather than interest. "I'm not eating here. I need to speak with the head chef for a moment, please." I could tell that the girl was immediately jealous. I was wearing a pair of dark Levi jeans with a V-neck white shirt and black blazer. I also had on curve cologne and my black and white Jordan 12's. I never stepped out looking like a clown. "Oh, my God! What do you want?" Shanice demanded quietly, as soon as she noticed it was me. "Can we talk, please, Miss I'll spend your money but not call?" I let her know that I knew she'd accepted my money because nothing was ever transferred back to me. "What, Dan? I'm at work," she whispered sharply, pulling me over to a corner where nobody could hear us. "Look, I know you hate me..." "Dan, hate would be the understatement of the year," she responded quickly, cutting me off. "Okay, I know that," I agreed, just to appease her. "But look, my mother is having a party Saturday night. Just come with me. If you do, I promise you'll see that a lot has changed." "No." "Shanice, please? Shit! It's the least you could do for taking my money and still acting like I don't exist. Please!" I said, trying to guilt her for leverage. "And if afterwards you never want to see or hear from me again, we can sign a contract and I'll disappear from your life completely." "One dinner party and I never have to hear from you again?" she said, weighing her options. "Yes," I agreed. I was confident she still loved me. She just needs to be reminded of what it's like to be Dan's girl. "What time should I be ready?" She looked excited at the thought of being rid of me for good, and I almost got offended. "A car will be here Saturday night around 6:00." "I'll be ready," she promised, turning to walk away without so much as a simple 'see ya later', but that was cool... she'd be mine again before the end of the night, come Saturday.

Chapter 54

MAXWELL

Here I was, standing in a club on a Tuesday... even though the club had never been my scene. As bad as I wanted to beat the hell out of Dan, I'd just recently received a call from him telling me about a dinner party his mom was throwing, but what really got my attention was when he said "Shanice is coming too, it'll be the three of us just like old times." It would be like old times alright. I didn't want to show up without a date though. I needed someone bad... someone who'd make Shanice come out of pocket in front of Dan so he'd know who really had her heart. So, after talking to one of the soldiers in my company who I knew for a fact was always going out, he recommended Club Juice because there would be a lot of females there on Tuesday, all because of the Chris Brown song called 'Tuesday'.

Apparently, the club was promoting ladies' drinks as free all night, and one dollar shots of Patron. I had been pissed when I found out the cover charge for guys was $25... he'd failed to mention that bit of information. Oh well, guess they had to make up for the lost money somewhere. I looked around the club, and noticed a very attractive mocha colored chick standing over in a corner by herself. You could tell this wasn't her scene either because she'd turned down the six guys that had approached her since I'd started watching. I decided to walk over and spark some conversation because she really was one of the baddest females I'd seen all night. She was around 5'6" with long pretty black hair that I hoped was natural, dark mysterious eyes, and lips that looked like pillows. "Hey," I smiled at her. "I'm not interested," she said, shooting me down before I'd even gotten started. "And who said I was?" I asked, determined to give her the same treatment. "You've been staring at me for close to an hour, you're interested," she was full of herself. "I'm really not," I smiled. "I've been staring at you for so long because you've been standing in this same spot, blocking my view of her." I pointed toward some random female who was standing near the DJ's table. "Oh, I'm sorry," she apologized. You could see the embarrassment all on her face and that did more than satisfy me. "Oh, it's cool. But since you did just act like a..." "Bitch?" she gasped, cutting me off. "You said it," I laughed. "Let me buy you a drink. Maybe we can talk and you could gain my interest... then, maybe I won't be thinking about her." "Sounds good," she laughed, following me over to the bar. We immediately hit it off. Her name was Nicole and she was a school teacher. This wasn't her normal scene but she was there looking out for a friend who'd just gone through a break-up. I hated that I was planning to use such a sweet woman, but I'd be sure to apologize later. I had to set my plan into play.

The Dinner Party Dandridge

I was so happy to have Shanice on my arm for my mother's dinner party! I knew my mother wouldn't approve but my sisters were just as excited, once I told them that I'd made the choice to follow my heart and not the advice of our mother. We always complimented each other so well. She wore a pair of black pants that fit just right, not too tight but not loose at all, with a sheer white top that showed just enough cleavage. I was pleased that she'd chosen the white spiked red bottom heels I'd gotten for her 25th birthday, while I wore the exact opposite but same colors. I had on a pair of white Levis with a white V-neck shirt and black vest. My shoes were all black, the Jordan 13's. We looked like a star couple. "Oh... Shanice," Mrs. Harris beamed, "what a pleasant surprise!" My mother was so fake. "How are you, Mrs. Harris?" Shanice was polite. "I'm doing okay," she answered. "I'm surprised you're not here with Maxwell. I heard you two are, well, a thing now." I knew my mother had gotten her information from Sharon so it didn't get to me at all, but what did get to me was the sad expression that seemed to pass across Shanice's face. "No, me and Maxwell are not a thing, but I'm happy to know you still care," she curtly responded to my mom before walking over to the table which held glasses of wine. "Must you start?" I asked my mother. "Must you continue to be seen with the trash?" she whispered, answering my question with another question. "Hi there, Dan." Without looking her way, Shanice knew it was Sharon's voice, and cringed, knowing she'd be expected to greet Sharon also. With a stiff lip, she forced a polite greeting. "Hey Sharon, how are you?" "I'm great, just getting big," she smiled, rubbing her small bulge and I wanted to throw up in my mouth. Sharon just knew she was having baby Maxwell ...and I knew different. "Well, good for you," I said before walking away. I did not want to deal with Sharon at all tonight. My focus for the evening would be catering to Shanice in any way possible so she'd be mine again by the end of the night. I looked over at the doorway and saw Maxwell stepping outside with his mother, her fiancé and a beautiful mocha colored female. It didn't take my boy no time to bounce back. I was proud of him!

Chapter 55

SHANICE

"Who is that?" I asked Dan when Maxwell and his date stepped outside to the pool area. "I guess that's Max's date," Dan answered. "She's pretty, huh?" I felt myself getting angry. Max and I had been together not even a full week ago, and he already had the next bitch on his arm. "What's going on Dan?" Max nodded politely, "Shanice?" He spoke casually as if this was a regular day between the three of us. "Nothing," I sighed, trying not to appear annoyed, "If you'll excuse me?" I decided this would be a good time to go to the bathroom and get away from them all, but I didn't even notice that Max was on my heels. "You cannot be in this bathroom with me," I challenged him, putting some force behind my words. "And... why not?" Max asked in a low sexy voice. "You said you were done with me, right?" I reminded him. I thought about making a comment about Sharon's presence at the party but decided against it. "Yeah." "Okay," I smiled, trying on purpose to be overly polite, "well, you should get back to your little date and be done... or is it two dates for you tonight? I noticed Sharon is in attendance too." He looked at me like he couldn't believe I was being so dismissive, but I couldn't believe he'd come with that girl and she had the nerve to be beautiful. I couldn't wait until Tameka showed up so I could vent to her, and not show my true feelings for Max in front of all these people. I walked back outside and saw Maxwell standing with her, laughing and giggling like nobody's business. I wanted to slap the taste out of his mouth. He kept shooting looks my way and I knew at that point, he was just trying to get under my skin... so I did the one thing I knew would really get under his.

Chapter 56

MAXWELL

I watched every move Shanice made, enjoying the look of envy that would come over her each time I laughed or smiled at something shared in the conversation between Nicole and myself. It was like watching someone set a fire ablaze and continuously add more gasoline to it. She was heated but she'd never admit it. I'd followed her to the bathroom, planning to give her one last chance to change her mind, but she'd dismissed me real quick. So, I figured, for the rest of the evening, I'd continue to play her little game. Shanice walked over to Dan, whispering something in his ear before kissing him. He smiled at the words she'd told him in secret and I began to see red. I stomped over to the edge of the pool where they were standing and, at that point, I had not a care in the world. She'd officially pissed me off. "So this is how you want to see things happen, huh!" I yelled at her for the first time ever. "Max! Calm down!" Shanice yelled back. I could tell she wasn't expecting the response she'd gotten from that kiss. "Calm down? I've got your calm!" I punched Dan in his jaw so hard; he fell back into the pool. "Is that calm enough for you?" I yelled. "What the hell, man?" Dan came up for air and I could tell he wanted to get out of the pool and go toe to toe! "You fucked up, Dan. That's what! Shanice belongs to me, has belonged to me ever since you broke her heart but she's so broken, so jaded... she can't give herself completely to anyone. Thank you!" "Thank me?" I could see the confusion written all over Dan's face. I was surprised that he hadn't already taken a swing at me. "Yes, thank you for your damaged goods!" I spat at him, hoping my words would cut him to the core. Before I could say another word, Shanice had slapped me. "That's what you think of me, Max! Damaged goods? Was I damaged when you were professing your love to me? Was I damaged when you were making love to me and planning our future?" "Yes, Shanice... you were." I was honest with her. I knew the confession would hurt her but at this point, I didn't care. "I'm out man," I added before turning to see Nicole staring in the direction of the fight. I lowered my head and walked over to her. "Look, I'm really sorry..." She put her hand up to stop my apology. "Don't worry about it, boo. We just met," she added, making me feel only slightly better, "no hard feelings." She walked away easy. I walked past my mom, who had the biggest look of disappointment on her face. I was not used to her looking at me that way. It hurt almost as much as knowing I would never be with Shanice ...not after today. I was sure we'd talk and things would be fine, eventually. I just wanted things to be fine with me and Shanice.

Chapter 57

SHANICE

I couldn't believe Max had just called me damaged goods, all because he couldn't have what he wanted. I watched as he headed for the door and Tameka stopped him. I had no idea what she'd just whispered to him, but I knew it involved me by the way he'd turned and looked my way. "What did you just say to him, Meka?" My sister seemed to be stuck in one place. La'Draysha began to clap her hands as if she'd already had this little fiasco all planned out. "Why are you clapping?" I asked her. "Because dear," she began, "now my son and Max both see you for what you really are, and the sad thing is, you'll never again be with either of them." I fought the tears that were stinging my eyes, which seemed to further fuel her tirade "Do you think these boys will choose you over their friendship?" she asked. "Maxwell already did," I challenged her. I looked at him because I wanted to him to speak up, I wanted to him to validate what I'd said. "Well, sorry but Maxwell can't be with you," Sharon chimed in. "And why is that?" Her presence was enough to put my nerves on edge but now, she was inserting herself into my conversation. "Because you can't be a stepmother to your own niece or nephew," she spoke proudly. I looked at Tameka whose eyes were full of tears, but I still wasn't getting it. "Niece or nephew?" I couldn't understand what Sharon was trying to say. "Oh my God! Are you that slow?" Sharon stared at me and I got that feeling again ...that she reminded me so much of Tameka. I looked between the two of them, again noticing how they were almost identical and it dawned on me. This bitch was saying she was my sister.

To Be Continued...

SNEAK PEEK

Teri Woods
presents
Having Your Brothers Back Can be The
My Brother's Keeper
Reason He Lives to See Another Day
Book IIII A Novel
ew York Times Be
Billie Dureyea Shell

MY BROTHER'S KEEPER

BOOK IIII

A Novel

Billie Dureyea Shell

Chapter 1

THE GENERAL

The General looked around his office, pondering his next move on the rebels. The rebel army had caused more problems within his smuggling business as of late. While he was out of the country trying to secure the African Black Diamond as his brother, also the South African president, had commanded. The rebels had raided his military artillery camps, taking whatever they could grab. He didn't receive any of the money promised from his brother because he'd failed to bring home the diamond. His next move had to be great, or the president would have his head put on a stake. The General watched people move about through his massive office window. He heard a knock at the door. He didn't bother walking over to ask who was interrupting his time of peace. "It's open, lieutenant." He continued to face the outside world. His mind moved to another place after the death of his father. The diamond was the cause of his murder, and the General would do anything to retrieve the precious stone, even if it meant going against his brother's rule. "General," the lieutenant stepped into the office. "My apologies for interrupting. I've come to ask how you wish to proceed with the rebels?" It was a question that he couldn't avoid with everything that had happened up until this point. Mainly with his brother putting an end to their field supplies. The army needed more weapons to deal with the rebels. He didn't have enough guns to supply all of his men. If he decided to move forward and attack the rebels, some would attend the battle without a weapon to fire. Instead, they would have to make use of knives, grenades, spears, or whatever they could construct to defend themselves. His army outnumbered the rebels, but the outcome would be intensely felt due to the number of casualties they would suffer in a war with another country. If only he had a replacement for Bill Right, the man he knew as Jar Simmons. "How would you like us to deal with the situation, Abrafo?" The General asked his most trusted comrade. For years, they had known each other since they were kids, training to become soldiers in the African military. The General excelled in war strategy while Abrafo exceeded in kills. And that's what his name stands for . . . executioner. The General gave Abrafo his name after learning about his family history. They were assassins, and the name Abrafo suited him well. It was the General's way of protecting his only friend's identity. "You are our leader," Lieutenant Abrafo replied. "It would be wise for you to give the command, not me. I am a man of war, and you are a man of approach. Your tactic will be far more effective than mine." The General turned from the window to face Abrafo. "Do you think it would be wise to start a war with the rebels?" The General wanted to test the lieutenant to see his view of their unfortunate circumstance. It didn't take long for Abrafo to understand what the General asked of him. The General wouldn't ask a third time for his opinion. "No, General." The answer was short, the way he intended for it to be, knowing a why question would follow. "Why do you feel as such?" The General asked curiously. Abrafo didn't become a high-ranking lieutenant by being a cretinous man. The army had to confront the rebels from a different standpoint, and the General needed a fresh perspective. Abrafo was more than a killer to him. He would be the General's new plan of action until his mind was off the diamond. He couldn't lead his men into a war without a clear sense of reason. "The rebels are growing strong in numbers," the lieutenant said evenly. "And they're confident now that they have successfully raided our camps for weapons. We will lose more soldiers than intended if we face them without first breaking their spirit." "Break their spirit," the General folded his hands behind his back. "And how would you suggest proceeding without a battle?" The lieutenant took a short moment to think about an answer. If he replied quickly, the General would possibly void his response. He looked to be deep in thought. His explanation had to be clear of mistakes and thoughtful. He spoke when formulating the right choice of words. "The same way you stop a fire-breathing dragon." The General smiled at Abrafo. "We cut off the head." Abrafo balled his first and placed it over his heart. "For Africa." The General followed suit. "For Africa."

KANE

"How much longer," Smoke sounded from the seat across from mine. "It's been hours, and my legs feel paralyzed." I looked back at my friend and smiled. Honestly, I was happy he could move his legs at all. Adrian had shot him in the leg, and Smoke had to use a cane to stand up straight for a week. At first, I thought he would never be the same, but that was just me worrying too much. My guy pulled through just fine. "It's not that bad," Kim said. "We'll get there in the next thirty minutes or so. Sit back and relax, crybaby." Smoke threw his head back on the seat rest, frustrated. I shook my head and turned my attention back to the map I had picked up in a store at the airport. We were on our way to Africa. Even Big Bruce decided to come with us. I told him it could get ugly, and he was still down to ride. None of us were in trouble with the law, so I booked a commercial flight straight to Tripoli, Libya. It cost me $1500 a ticket. Not that it mattered, but damn, I know now why people save money for vacations. This was my first time leaving the country, and it felt good to get away even though I was traveling to find my mother. I didn't have my father's black notebook anymore. It would've been helpful because it had names and locations. The only thing I had to lean on was the map in my father's office. There were pinned locations that corresponded with the notebook. That's how I figured out my mother would be somewhere in Libya. It's where my father built his organization and headquarters. Where I assume he stored the money and weapons. The only thing I couldn't figure out was why my mother chose Jordan over me? We could've done this together. "How long are you gonna stare at that map?" Kim asked. "What are you trying to figure out that we don't know already?" "Roads, places," I gave her a short answer. "Studying the landscape." "Why," she asked and leaned her head against my shoulder. "One, I think it'd be best if I at least know where we're at," I informed her. "And two, I'm searching for an unoccupied area away from the city. Somewhere, a plane can land without being noticed by the army." "I thought your father worked with the army?" I looked around and saw several people staring at us. Mostly Africans, heading back to their homeland after visiting America. After Kim said, your father worked with the army; we caught ugly glares from everyone who heard. "Keep your voice down," I whispered. "I don't think foreigners should be talking about the army." She secretly looked around and spotted the people with hard eyes on us. "Right." "Anyway," I began. "I wasn't talking about Libya's army. I was talking about rebel armies who'd love to get their hands on money and weapons. My father would've avoided those areas to prevent any problems." "What if he paid them off," she remembered to speak with a low voice. "It's possible," I said. "But why spend extra money when you can just stay off the grid?" My father wouldn't work with them knowing they were against the army—too much of a headache." "For you," she replied. "I think like him," I smiled. "Whatever, smart guy," she kissed my cheek. I believe it to be true that my father wouldn't work with a malicious group. The notebook had names of Generals and prominent figures written in it. He was larger than life, and it would take more than a few soldiers to protect what he built. He used to tell me, don't work hard at something if you're gonna half-ass in the end? I wouldn't do it, so why would he? The only thing I ever smuggled was contraband from one cell to another when I was locked up. The guards didn't allow inmates to trade anything, so we had to move low-key. I met a guy who would watch my cell while I was on free time for a pack of cigarettes a week. Inmates would sneak into your cell and steal goods while you were away watching TV or occupied in the yard. After it happened to me once, I knew that I had to hire help. I paid a killer to watch over other inmates with sticky fingers, and it worked. This situation was no different. My father hired the army so he could move freely on the land, but that didn't mean the rebels wouldn't try their hand. If you build a restaurant around rats, they'll eat your food. That's how I look at it. And . . . there are plenty of rats where we're going, if you know what I mean.

Chapter 3

ABEL

Abel checked his watch and smiled. Silva had successfully landed the plane in Africa. They had touchdown just past the border of Mali. Abel looked around the area through the side window and saw the desert go on for miles. The sand and dirt covering the area appeared to be endless, and he had already begun to feel the heat beaming down from the sun. He stood when the plane came to a complete stop, opting to sit in the back to keep a close eye on Silva and Britt. "How hot is it?" Gina stood and wiped the sweat from her forehead. The heat made her want to ask Silva to fly them back home. She had never experienced a high temperature at this level, and it was more than enough to get her frustrated. "It's one hundred and five degrees," Snake answered exasperatedly.

"What the fuck," Gina muttered at nobody in particular. "I'm getting woozy," Bam stood and dropped back into the seat. "I don't know if I can do this. It's too hot for me to think straight." Gina formed a disgusted expression on her face when she looked at Bam. It was her moment to comment on his weakness, but receiving a response would've gotten her even angrier in combination with the sun. The heat provided her enough irritation to deal with for now. "Get yourself together," Abel told Bam before opening the plane's side door. He immediately felt a strong breeze of heat attack his entire body as if an unknown entity forced it. The fury of wind lasted a short span before he was able to step off the aircraft. Abel held up his hand and spotted a large dome tent and a 4x4 off-road jeep. The campsite appeared invisible from the air. It was the perfect color for someone who wished to camouflage it with the surrounding landscape. Silva turned off the engine and followed the others off the plane. He stood next to Abel and pointed at the dome tent. "Dat a ih." Mali was the closest destination Silva could land without the army noticing the aircraft. Abel knew this to be true with the amount of illegal activity that had taken place throughout the years. If he desired a safe and secure landing, Mali was the only option without the plane getting shot down. He turned to Bam and Snake. "Unload the supplies." Bam spoke up, "What about her?" his eyes were on Gina, wondering why Abel didn't ask her to help. "Shut up, you idiot," Snake eyed Bam. Abel didn't bother to turn around when he spoke. "I want you to be alive when I return." Bam was mind-boggled with Abel's response. His words rang out in his mind . . . I want you to be alive when I return. Bam planned to murder Gina before leaving America, and he knew that she carried the same intentions. Abel was right. They couldn't be left alone together, not even for a second. He sucked his teeth and followed Snake back inside the plane. Gina smirked at Bam as he turned away, thinking his time would come. Keep on, tough guy, she thought. Hiding her anger toward Bam was becoming a daily task. When Abel no longer needs Bam, he's dead. He was at the top of her to-kill list, without a doubt. Britt stepped beside Abel. "I noticed you're in pain while on the plane. Is everything alright with you?" She had a concerned look on her face. Gina bumped Britt out of her way and stood next to Abel. "He's fine," she snarled. "Let's go inside. It's fucking hot out here." She held Abel's arm and guided him toward the tent. Silva witnessed the tension between Gina and Britt. He was still unaware of how Britt felt about Abel. She hadn't shown any signs of feelings for him until now. "Blurtnawt," he muttered, walking past Britt. Abel stopped at the tent's door, waiting for Silva to catch up and lead the way inside. "After you," he smiled at Silva as if opening the door would spring a trap. "Yah mon," Silva pulled back the opening, showing there was nothing to fear. After stepping inside, he called to the man sitting Indian-style on a throw rug in front of them. "Oyoo." Oyoo opened his eyes and stared at them. He had a mean expression on his face as though they disrupted his concentration while meditating. After a short moment of studying the other unknown guests, he smiled at his friend. "Silva," Oyoo sounded excited and stood to greet him. Abel stood firm by the door with Gina as the two men shook hands. He kept his eyes on Oyoo the entire time while on high alert. If he missed any potential threats, Gina would take care of it. That's why he wanted her to come inside with him. Her awareness was greater than Bam and Snake's put together, which kept him at ease. Oyoo looked over Silva's shoulder and spoke. "That man reminds me of someone. Who is he?" Silva turned around and faced Abel. "Di dead mon son." Oyoo's eyes widened. "Jar," he said in shock. He stepped closer to Abel. "Have you come to take his place?" Oyoo noticed Abel's muscular physique, and the man was by far larger than his father. Oyoo worked with Jar for more than twenty years as a driver. When beginning the smuggling business, Silva and Oyoo were Jar's first transportation hires. Jar cared for them to the point that there wasn't a need to work for anyone else. Even after Jar's death, the men were well off, but they loved making money and stayed in business as contractors for anyone looking to transport. Abel scanned Oyoo as he approached, noticing he was a man of the land who could speak perfect English. He was surprised by that and how well kept it was inside the tent. He expected it to be dusty and hot. It was neither, and somehow the sun rays didn't affect the inside temperature. "I haven't decided as of yet." "Then why have you come, son of Jar?" Oyoo looked at Abel's chest and felt his pain. It was a gift he possessed that allowed him to sense the aura surrounding the body. "I've come for the General," Abel answered truthfully. "I have a gift for him." Oyoo smiled sarcastically. "A gift for the General. The man who brings war to his people." Oyoo turned away from Abel. "What gift do you bring, if not weapons? He values his army, and your father made a business of it. Your gift will get you killed." "I beg to differ," Abel said confidently. "I have something he's been searching for." Oyoo turned around and thought, could he possibly have it? There was only one thing the General would accept besides weapons. And that would be the African Black Diamond. He was well aware of the rebels raiding the campsites. The General announced that anyone who worked with the rebels would be killed. "You have it?" Abel signed with a slight nod. "Okay, I will lead you to the General, but I will not reveal myself," Oyoo said, hiding his true intentions. He pointed to Abel's chest. "I will show you to a doctor before we go. You will need all of your strength, son of Jar."

JORDAN

Noti looked at the surrounding area and noticed a plane at their landing spot. It's been several years since she returned to the landing zone. It was one of many locations Jar used for travel. She remembered meeting Oyoo with her husband at a bar in Bamako. Oyoo worked as a tour guide and offered to show them around the city. Jar accepted, and the next day Oyoo picked them up from a hotel. They toured the entire town, and Jar was impressed with Oyoo's sense of direction and driving skills. It was enough for Jar to extend a proposal for Oyoo to be part of the business. Noti thought about landing the plane anyway but quickly decided it wouldn't be a good idea. Her husband was dead, and she figured Oyoo had found a new boss. Nobody knew who she was except

Oyoo, and whoever it was visiting might not be friendly. They were in dangerous waters, and steering clear of violence was the key to staying alive a day longer. "We need to land at another location." "I thought this was the location," Adrian spoke up from the pilot's seat. "I don't see anywhere else to land." Rick sat in the back of the plane next to Jordan. He'd never been more terrified in his life. Jordan and his brother Adrian were monsters. After Jordan woke up, he became himself again, and the FBI agent was gone. He lashed out at Adrian for knocking him over the head. Adrian could've wrecked the plane if Noti and Rick didn't stop him in time. Jordan kept his eyes on his brother for most of the trip. Rick thought if he closed his eyes for a second, they all be dead. Sleep was not an option either, and he damn near didn't blink. "Land this fucking plane," Jordan growled at Adrian. "You said this was the spot, and now you've changed your mind all of a sudden. That's not gonna work for me. This flight is over." He stared at Noti hard. She somehow became the bandleader, which didn't sit right with him. She'd be useless if he could get her to give up the safe location and the passcode. Striking that kind of luck would end her life, and he knew it wouldn't happen. He'd never get the information, not if she desired to live. Jordan's frustration dictated his actions, and until he regained control of the situation, his goal was to piss them off. "Never mind the plane," Noti said evenly. "And prepare yourself for a fight. That's the only option if we land now." "She's right," Rick spoke up. He noticed the aircraft and spotted two men unloading luggage. "Well, we have to land soon," Adrian checked the gasoline level meter. "We're running short on fuel." They had to miss a fuel station because a police boat docked nearby. He couldn't risk it and let the last opportunity pass by. Jordan began to spaz out, letting his emotion run wild. "Fuck!" he roared and started to destroy anything in reach. "How are we runnin' short on fuel?" He tossed random items to the front of the plane. He picked up a glass of water and threw it at the front window, just missing Adrian. "Goddammit!" "Someone calm his ass down," Adrian shouted and took a split second to glance back at Jordan. That would've been the last straw if the glass hit him. Jordan was pushing it to the maximum limit, and Adrian was more than ready to do something harmful to his brother, even if it meant ending his arrangement with Noti. Rick turned his attention from the plane below and focused on his former partner. "Shit," he muttered and tried to defuse Jordan's outrage. He held up his hands and blocked Jordan from throwing more items toward the cockpit. "Are you trying to kill us?" "Get the hell out of my way, Rick." Jordan had the devil inside of him and wasn't afraid to show it. The Planner was the cause of his outrage. It wasn't his fault the plane was running out of fuel. It wasn't his fault Noti was the one in control. It wasn't his fault Rick had to tag along with them. So many different things began to fester inside his head, and he wanted to break loose. Freeing himself from everyone and unleashing his anger was the only way to do it. It made him feel good, and Rick kept trying to stop that sensation. "I can't let you distract your brother from landing this plane safely." Rick kept his hands up and continued to block Jordan's path. Why did I get myself into this, he thought. He wouldn›t be in this predicament if he only called for backup when discovering the cabin. Obey the rules as an officer and follow protocol. That's all it takes, and he failed to do both when Adrian apprehended him in the woods. Jordan suddenly felt exhausted, and he just stood there, staring at Rick like a madman. His chest heaved in and out, taking in deep breaths of air. He needed water before he passed out from dehydration. It was hot, and his energy output didn't agree with the heat from the sun. He looked at the cooler on the side of the seat. Hopefully, there was another bottle of water inside. He reached for it, and Rick reacted by moving in his way. "Get the hell out of my way. I need a drink." Rick sighed and looked at the cooler. "Okay," he moved to the side. Jordan opened the cooler and cracked open a water bottle. He tossed the cap at Rick's chest, and it bounced off to the ground. He smirked at him, "Rookie." The whole time Jordan was having a fit, Noti focused on the plane below. The men appeared to be Americans. Maybe they were smugglers who prospered after her husband's death. When a king is dead, a new one will rise in any case. The luggage couldn't carry the number of weapons it takes to feed one rebel group. There could be a second plane, or money was in the bags. Suddenly, a woman and Oyoo emerged from the tent. Her eyes were sharp enough to assure it was him. She learned to see from a flying distance in the beginning stages of Jar's operation. He wasn't the only one taking risks for their future. It can't be, she thought. Another figure emerged from the dome tent. Noti was stunned after realizing a demon had followed her to Africa. As the plane passed over the location, she could've sworn Abel looked into the aircraft and made eye contact with her. She fell back from the window in shock. Her heart rate began to speed up a notch, and she felt like it would explode. Abel could have caused her to have a mild heart attack. She put her hand over her chest in fear. Rick caught her from falling to the ground before speaking to her worriedly. "Are you okay?" "No," she answered seriously. "The devil has arrived."

ABOUT THE AUTHOR

New York Times & International Best Selling Author
Billie Dureyea Shell was born in Compton California and now
lives in Ladera Heights with his wife and
kids who he loves to spend time with.
He is the Owner of several properties in the Los Angeles area
and gives back to his community by providing low income
housing to those who need it.
He stated "It doesn't matter where you at or where you from
it's what you do with your time. There's nothing you can't do
if you put your mind to it".